Sketches of Young Ladies

Young Gentlemen

AND

Young Couples

CHARLES DICKENS

---◆---

Sketches

OF

Young Gentlemen

AND

Young Couples

---◆---

WITH

Sketches of Young Ladies

BY

EDWARD CASWALL

---◆---

ILLUSTRATED BY

PHIZ

OXFORD
UNIVERSITY PRESS

OXFORD
UNIVERSITY PRESS

Great Clarendon Street, Oxford OX2 6DP

Oxford University Press is a department of the University of Oxford.
It furthers the University's objective of excellence in research, scholarship,
and education by publishing worldwide in

Oxford New York

Auckland Cape Town Dar es Salaam Hong Kong Karachi
Kuala Lumpur Madrid Melbourne Mexico City Nairobi
New Delhi Shanghai Taipei Toronto

With offices in

Argentina Austria Brazil Chile Czech Republic France Greece
Guatemala Hungary Italy Japan Poland Portugal Singapore
South Korea Switzerland Thailand Turkey Ukraine Vietnam

Oxford is a registered trade mark of Oxford University Press
in the UK and in certain other countries

Published in the United States
by Oxford University Press Inc., New York

British Library Cataloguing in Publication Data

Data available

Library of Congress Cataloging in Publication Data

Library of Congress Control Number: 2011934717

Typeset by RefineCatch Limited, Bungay, Suffolk
Printed in Great Britain
on acid-free paper by
Clays Ltd, St Ives plc

ISBN 978–0–19–960328–2

1 3 5 7 9 10 8 6 4 2

Contents

Introduction

By the summer of 1837 Charles Dickens had shot to fame 'like a rocket' (in the words of an early reviewer[1]) and was well on his way to becoming the hottest literary property of the century. *Sketches by Boz*, which collected in three volumes the newspaper and magazine pieces he had been producing piecemeal since 1833, had been published in two series in February and December 1836 to rapturous reviews, and *The Pickwick Papers*, commissioned in response to that first success, was appearing in its fifteenth monthly serial part, to even greater acclaim. *Oliver Twist* had begun its monthly run in the pages of *Bentley's Miscellany*, which Dickens was editing. By then he had also written and produced three plays and an anonymous pamphlet, but it was his serial publications which were the primary sensation.

Eager to expand their fledgling company and to exploit the success of their star writer, Chapman and Hall, the publishers of *Pickwick*, brought out a collection of brief vignettes called *Sketches of Young Ladies*, by a pseudonymous author, 'Quiz', with engravings by Hablot Browne ('Phiz'). It sold splendidly, having reached its eighth edition within just over a year, and Dickens, writing anonymously (he was under contract to Richard Bentley, his *Oliver Twist* publisher, not to bring out anything additional with a rival publisher), six months later produced a sequel, *Sketches of Young Gentlemen*, which also

[1] Abraham Hayward, *Quarterly Review*, 59 (Oct. 1837), 484–518.

did very well, going through five editions in ten months. Two years later, in 1840, Dickens, his imagination piqued by the queen's announcement of her engagement to Prince Albert, composed a third volume in the series, *Sketches of Young Couples*, again published anonymously. The three titles were gathered together in a single volume in 1843 and again in 1869 and 1875, by which time Dickens was dead. His authorship of the latter two titles was revealed in John Forster's *Life of Charles Dickens* (1872–4). The identity of Edward Caswall as Quiz was not disclosed until a biographical sketch appeared in a collection of his hymns in 1908, long after his death in 1878. By that time and until now the three little books disappeared almost without trace, rarely reprinted and almost never meriting more than a line or two from critics or biographers. It is the purpose of the present volume to rectify that disappearance; in the words of a late nineteenth-century reader of these sketches, 'there is yet gold to be got out of Dickens'.[2]

The journalistic format of short fiction, essays, sketches, serials, and miscellaneous writings was very much the dominant mode of publication in the 1830s. Whereas Sir Walter Scott's Waverley novels, commencing in 1814, had led the ascendancy of works of long fiction in the early nineteenth century, the publication of novels declined dramatically following the bankruptcy in 1826 of the firms of Archibald Constable and James Ballantyne, publisher and printer respectively of Scott's works. In place of novels, a veritable deluge of sketch writing flooded the field in the 1820s and 1830s, both as single pieces in newspapers and magazines,

[2] *York Herald*, 15 Mar. 1884.

and as collections in volumes. Writers largely forgotten today, such as Theodore Hook, Thomas Hood, John Poole, and Robert Surtees, produced sketches which competed with the longer-lasting achievements of Washington Irving's *Sketch Book* (1819–20), Mary Russell Mitford's *Our Village* (1824–32), William Makepeace Thackeray's *Paris Sketch Book* (1840)—and of Dickens's works. It is this context which underlies the publication of all of Dickens's novels as monthly or weekly serials, as he developed his own distinctive talents within the publishing conditions of his day.

But that is to jump ahead. By 1837 Dickens had written sixty sketches as Boz;[3] *Pickwick* was initially a series of set-piece scenes, plus interpolated stories, and *Oliver Twist* has long been recognized as an extended version of the 'Our Parish' sketches which filled the opening pages of the final arrangement of *Sketches by Boz*. As a distinctive form, the sketch (as its name implies) is closely related to graphic illustration. It has a strongly visual outlook, with descriptions of physical characteristics often used to represent abstract moral qualities. It is often accompanied by engravings, which, participating in the same tradition, provide singularly apt complement to the written words. The illustrations for *Sketches by Boz* were executed by George Cruikshank, the foremost caricaturist and illustrator of the day, and those for *Sketches of Young Ladies*, *Gentlemen*, and *Couples* were undertaken by Browne, the illustrator of *Pickwick* and of most later titles by Dickens. Cruikshank and Browne both followed in the footsteps of

[3] Dickens's first six sketches were published without a byline, and his contributions to *Bell's Life* were originally attributed to 'Tibbs', but once collected these sketches have always afterwards been described as the work of Boz. Eight sketches were combined into four in collected editions, making the final total fifty-six.

Introduction

Dickens's favourite artist, William Hogarth, to whose engravings Dickens's writings are often compared. Invariably short and generally non-narrative (although there are notable exceptions in *Sketches by Boz* and elsewhere), the sketch provides no more (and no less) than an observant glance at a scene or character. In graphic art the sketch is often preliminary to a more elaborate painting, and the sense of unfinished spontaneity, which is a key component of its attraction, is also testimony to the authenticity of its realism.[4] The subjects of literary sketching are generally contemporary, viewed through a satirical perspective by a genial onlooker, who is at once detached and caught up in the scene which he describes. Following Walter Benjamin's analysis of Baudelaire, the speaker in a sketch is often seen as a *flâneur*, or stroller, who saunters observantly through an urban setting. Recent criticism, however, rejects this interpretation of the observer as a bohemian outsider, considering him instead 'one of a countless number of ordinary city-dwellers who read metropolitan surfaces', an image which provides singularly apt description of the persona of the speakers in *Sketches of Young Ladies*, *Gentlemen*, and *Couples*.[5]

The first of these three little works, *Sketches of Young Ladies*, was written by a young literary aspirant, Edward Caswall (1814–78). As an undergraduate at Brasenose College, Oxford, Caswall neglected his studies to produce 'The Oxonian', a series of sketches published in the *Metropolitan*

---

[4] Alison Byerly, 'Effortless Art: The Sketch in Nineteenth-Century Painting and Literature', *Criticism*, 41 (1999), 349–64.

[5] Martina Lauster, *Sketches of the Nineteenth Century: European Journalism and its Physiologies, 1830–50* (Houndsmills: Palgrave Macmillan, 2007), 9.

Magazine in 1835, and *A New Art Teaching How to be Plucked* (1835), a wittily facetious pamphlet setting forth instructions on how to fail university examinations.[6] After graduating with second-class honours, he won a scholarship for two further years of study and was subsequently awarded an MA (1838). In addition to *Sketches of Young Ladies*, he wrote *Morals from the Churchyard* (1838), a Christian allegory for children which bears striking similarity in some of its core elements to *The Old Curiosity Shop* (1840–1), Dickens's story of the exemplary life and death of Little Nell.[7] The popular success of *Young Ladies* led Caswall to consider a literary career, and he wrote a sequel on young gentlemen, but 'put it aside in favour of the ministry'.[8] He took orders in 1839, converted to Roman Catholicism in 1847, and after the death of his wife entered the Oratory in Birmingham, where he was ordained a Catholic priest in 1852. He achieved some fame as the author and translator of many hymns, and has been the subject of a recent biography.[9]

Having adopted the pseudonym 'Scriblerus Redivivus' ('the satirical writer come back to life') for *Pluck*, for *Sketches of Young Ladies* Caswall called himself 'Quiz', a name indicating a witty fellow who mocks or ridicules. The sketches consist of twenty-four brief descriptions of a variety of types

[6] It was a popular success, with new editions appearing throughout the century under variant titles—*A New Art Teaching How to be Plucked*, *Pluck Examination Papers*, and *The Art of Pluck*.

[7] See Paul Schlicke, 'The True Pathos of *The Old Curiosity Shop*', *Dickens Quarterly*, 7 (1990), 189–99.

[8] Edward Ballasis, 'Biographical Note on the Rev. Edward Caswall', in Caswell's *Hymns and Poems Original and Translated* (London: Burns & Oates, 1908), 6.

[9] Nancy Marie De Flon, *Edward Caswall: Newman's Brother and Friend* (Leominster: Gracewing, 2005).

of contemporary young middle-class females, described by an adolescent male, Mr. P——, whose observations are based mainly on witnessing young women at social gatherings. There is only occasionally any of the individuation which makes Dickens's character sketches so memorable, and each sketch concludes with a moral assessment of the subject under scrutiny. But the content and manner of these sketches led admiring reviewers to praise them as 'rather droll' (*York Herald*, 8 July 1837) and 'pleasing' (*Hull Packet*, 14 July 1837). 'In many respects these caricatures come so nearly to life', wrote another reviewer, 'that we humbly think some young ladies might here and there find a hint for the improvement of their habits or their manners' (*Sheffield Independent*, 19 August 1837).

The Preface, attributed to M. P.—initials with no known referent—announces the purpose of the work, namely to set forth the classification of young ladies according to the Linnæan system, a 'philosophical theme' which, he ironically laments, has been neglected by the foremost authorities of the age, and which (he maintains) has been erroneously described by another. The Linnæan system is a methodology established by Carl Linnæus, the Swedish botanist and zoologist, who founded modern taxonomy and binomial nomenclature, and the authorities Caswall accuses of neglect of his important subject are among the foremost scientists of the age. Georges Cuvier, Dionysius Lardner, and Mary Somerville had all published notable works on aspects of natural history and the physical sciences. And Caswall facetiously accuses William Buckland, dean of Westminster, the author of the first account of a dinosaur fossil and a leading proponent of creationism, of the error of mistaking troglodytes for ichthyosauri. In fact,

Buckland writes learnedly about the ichthyosaurus, an extinct giant marine reptile resembling a fish (the first fossilized remains were found in 1811 by Mary Annig in Lyme Regis), but not at all about troglodytes, or cavemen.

On the face of it, Caswall is indulging in hifalutin banter, proposing that his whimsical descriptions of young ladies constitute learned enquiry of importance equal to the great scientific advances of the era. In light of Caswall's later career, however, one can detect a serious purpose beneath the ridicule. At the time he was writing, scientific investigations into geological and fossil remains were causing great alarm to thoughtful Christians, who feared the discoveries as a radical challenge to the veracity of the biblical account of creation, as set down in the Book of Genesis. Proofs that the earth and its plants and creatures had existed for millennia seemed flatly to contradict the Mosaic tradition, which holds that God had relatively recently created the world and its creatures in seven days. To confront this apparent contradiction, Francis Egerton, the eighth earl of Bridgewater (1756–1829), inspired by William Paley's *Natural Theology; or, Evidences of the Existence and Attributes of the Deity* (1802), commissioned eight 'Bridgewater Treatises' to explore 'the Power, Wisdom, and Goodness of God, as manifested in the Creation'.

The sixth of the Bridgewater Treatises was Buckland's *Geology and Mineralogy Considered with Reference to Natural Theology* (1836). Buckland declared that it was

matter of surprise that learned and religious men regard with suspicion and jealousy the study of natural phenomena, which abound with proofs of the highest attributes of the deity . . . No reasonable man [he maintained] can doubt that all the phenomena of the natural world derive their origin from God; and no one who believes the Bible to be the word of God, has cause to fear a discrepancy between this, his word, and the results of any discoveries respecting the nature of his works. (pp. 8–9)

For a devout Christian such as Caswall, such reassurance must have been extraordinarily comforting, and therefore for him to burlesque Buckland's work, as he does, attests to his confidence that the human race can be seen to fit comfortably within the beneficence of God's creation. His approach closely mirrors that of Buckland: in his disquisition on ichthyosauri Buckland states that: 'As it will be foreign to our purpose to enter on details respecting species I shall content myself with referring to the figures of the four most common forms' (p. 170); in limiting himself to twenty-four types of young lady, Quiz explains that he will endeavour 'to discover in the youthful fair certain latent characteristics, under which all the young ladies of this age and country might be classed, without describing each in particular' (p. 6).

In one of the rare modern discussions of *Sketches of Young Ladies* Martina Lauster dismisses Caswall's purported claim of scientific examination, proposing that 'Quiz's sympathies do not lie with the advance of knowledge at the expense of traditional gender roles, but with Buckland's religious conservatism'. Conservative Caswall indubitably is, but it misreads his humorous intentions to suppose that he is seriously concerned with 'the advance of knowledge', and it is historically anachronistic to maintain that the classification of young ladies 'serves as an outlet for misogyny'.[10] Caswall holds women in contempt no more than Milton does in *Paradise Lost*; rather, like Milton he accepts with relief the

---

[10] Lauster, *Sketches of the Nineteenth Century*, 124–8.

received wisdom of the ages regarding gender roles: just as Satan should not aspire to equality with God, so a woman can be most perfect not by trying to be like a man but by finding purpose and fulfilment within her own proper sphere. Caswall celebrates the liveliness and variety of women's behaviour, gently mocking their silliness and cheerfully encouraging their virtues.

Following on the success of Caswall's little book, *Sketches of Young Gentlemen* purports to offer a riposte to the 'slander' which the Dedicator of the later work claims was directed by Quiz at the fair sex, and at least one modern reader accepts that prefatory declaration at face value.[11] The mock formality of the Preface seems to me to indicate, however, how firmly Dickens's tongue is in his cheek. The irony is confirmed by his complaints that it was 'not polite' of Quiz to refer to young ladies as animals, even though they are such, and that 'Troglodites' is a 'hard word' which may or may not be 'injurious and disrespectful', for all anyone can be expected to know. Instead of being an 'antidote' to *Sketches of Young Ladies*, *Sketches of Young Gentlemen* instead carries forward the same lightly mocking tone, directed once more at young ladies as well as at young gentlemen.

Sketches of Young Gentlemen differs in basic respects from *Sketches of Young Ladies*, however, and although the book's first readers did not recognize the hand of Boz (nor did Dickens ever publicly acknowledge the sketches as his own), already distinctively Dickensian touches are evident—as they emphatically are not in a rival publication, the jejune *Characteristic Sketches of Young Gentlemen*, by Quiz,

[11] Valerie Browne Lester, *Phiz: The Man Who Drew Dickens* (London: Chatto & Windus, 2004), 71–2.

Junior.[12] In the first place, although Dickens's sequel is of nearly identical length to *Young Ladies*, it contains only half as many portraits (twelve as opposed to twenty-four). The expansion of canvas provides Dickens with scope to introduce the marvellously lively imaginative details which constitute the hallmark of his characterization. Introduced into specific situations, the figures are individuated even as they stand for representative types. Thus the Domestic Young Gentleman, who wears his handkerchief 'in the right-hand pocket of his great-coat', 'sneezed four times and coughed once after being out in the rain'. The excessive precision enforces the comedy. The Bashful Young Gentleman, having overset the bread at the dinner table, 'played with it a little, as gentlemen in the streets may be seen to do with their hats on a windy day, and then giving the roll a smart rap in his anxiety to catch it, knocked it with great adroitness into a tureen of white soup at some distance'. The comparison heightens the absurdity of his already farcical behaviour. The Military Young Gentleman is admired for his red coat—even though firemen, unnoticed by the ladies, wear 'not only red coats but very resplendent and massive badges besides'. Here, both the ladies and the gentlemen come in for Boz's genial mockery.

Like *Sketches by Boz*, *Sketches of Young Gentlemen* is laced with topical allusion, much with personal resonance (sometimes prescient) for Dickens. The Political Young Gentleman considers Harriet Martineau, the political economist who later contributed to *Household Words*, 'the greatest woman who ever lived'. The Poetical Young

---

[12] William Kidd, publisher of *Characteristic Sketches*, advertised that his was the original work, 'fraudulently imitated', he claimed, by the Chapman & Hall volume (*Operative*, 4 Nov. 1838).

Gentleman resembles Richard John Smith (known as 'O' Smith after Obi, his role in *Three-Fingered Jack*), the actor famed for the diabolical laugh of his melodramatic villains, who was shortly to take on the Dickensian roles of Fagin and Noggs at the Adelphi Theatre. The Theatrical Young Gentleman admires 'Miss Sheriff' (*sic*; actually Jane Shirreff), an accomplished soprano who performed at Drury Lane and Covent Garden and who sang alongside Dickens's sister Fanny in the 1834 Westminster Abbey Festival. And the Young Ladies' Young Gentleman goes with the ladies to a picnic at Chigwell, which Dickens told Forster was 'the greatest place in the world'.[13]

The fullest and most fulsome review of *Sketches of Young Gentlemen* praised the book's merit, judiciously identifying the sources of its appeal:

The wit and cleverness of this little volume have surprised us—we were quite unprepared for so much genuine humour, and capital knowledge of life, in a shape so unpretending. The tone is that of ridicule, but ridicule applied to its proper objects and never misplaced or unjust. The humanities of comic license, if we may so speak, are pleasantly preserved. The writer, whoever he is, is thoroughly 'up' to his subject—has looked about the world with a very clear perception of what is going on in it—sketches the humorous sides of character with careless but graphic ease—and seems incapable of any worse feeling than that of great animal spirits in connection with sincere goodheartedness. He pampers his jokes now and then into extravagance, and they are none the worse for it. People of only moderate relish, or with a turn for shallow gravity, will avoid this book.[14]

---

[13] *The Letters of Charles Dickens*, ed. Madeline House, Graham Storey, *et al.*, The British Academy/Pilgrim Edition (Oxford: Clarendon Press, 1965–2002), i. 243.　　　　[14] *Examiner*, 4 Feb. 1838.

Introduction

The fact that this estimate appeared in the *Examiner*, whose literary editor (and almost certainly the contributor of the review) was Dickens's intimate friend John Forster, should have given the game away, but the author's identity remained unknown for the rest of his life.

Later critics, when they have noticed *Sketches of Young Gentlemen* at all, have often been disparaging of what Duane DeVries stigmatizes as 'pedestrian work hurriedly written'. K. J. Fielding dismisses the volume as 'absurd essays'. I cannot agree; Peter Ackroyd seems to me to judge more accurately when he speaks of 'sharp and well-sustained comic sketches in which Dickens characteristically turns human beings into various "types" in the approved early nineteenth-century manner'. And Michel Slater celebrates the 'joyous caricature' of the Theatrical Young Gentleman, shrewdly noting that 'the contemporary theatre and its conventions . . . inspire some of his best comic touches'.[15] In some of these sketches we can see foreshadowing of some of Dickens's great comic figures: the poetical John Chivery, the domestic Tom Pinch, the bashful Augustus Moddle, the throwing-off Alfred Mantalini, and above all the theatrical Richard Swiveller.

Without doubt, the form of the sketch appealed to Dickens, not only in his later creation of journalistic figures such as Joe Whelks and Mr Booley, but more proximately in the volume he published (again anonymously) two years to the day after

---

[15] Duane DeVries, *Dickens's Apprentice Years: The Making of a Novelist* (Brighton: Harvester, 1976), 52; K. J. Fielding, *Charles Dickens: A Critical Introduction* (London: Longmans, 1958), 45; Peter Ackroyd, *Dickens* (London: Sinclair-Stevenson, 1990), 241; Michael Slater, *Charles Dickens* (New Haven: Yale University Press, 2009), 113.

Young Gentlemen, during the gap between his completion of *Nicholas Nickleby* and the commencement of *The Old Curiosity Shop*. *Sketches of Young Couples* was published on 10 February 1840 to coincide with the marriage of the young Queen Victoria to her cousin Albert of Saxe-Coburg. Their engagement, publicly announced on 23 November 1839, wildly stirred Dickens's imagination, and for several days he indulged, with Quilp-like extravagance, in the hilarious pretence that he was himself madly in love with the queen.

Society is unhinged here, by her majesty's marriage, and I am sorry to add [he wrote to W. S. Landor] that I have fallen hopelessly in love with the Queen, and wander up and down with vague and dismal thoughts of running away to some uninhabited island with a maid of honor, to be entrapped by conspiracy for that purpose.[16]

And to Forster he wrote:

The presence of my wife aggravates me. I loathe my parents. I detest my house. I begin to have thoughts of the Serpentine, of the regent's-canal, of the razors upstairs, of the chemist's down the street, of poisoning myself at Mrs. ——'s table, of hanging myself upon the pear-tree in the garden, of abstaining from food and starving myself to death, of being bled for my cold and tearing off the bandage, of falling under the feet of cab-horses in the New-road, of murdering Chapman and Hall and becoming great in story (SHE must hear something of me then—perhaps sign the warrant: or is that a fable?) of turning Chartist, of heading some bloody assault upon the palace and saving Her by my single hand—of being anything but what I have been, and doing anything but what I have done.[17]

The volume is prefaced by a facetious 'Urgent Remonstrance', in parody of the Grand Remonstrance of 1641 which

---

[16] *Letters*, ii. 23.   [17] Ibid. 24.

precipitated the English Civil War. Protesting that the queen's example, in a leap year, will incite young ladies to entrap eligible bachelors into matrimony, and instancing the recent marriage of the foreign secretary and future prime minister Henry John Temple, later Viscount Palmerston, as further incitement to such 'outrages', Dickens urges her to 'take immediate steps' to avert such dangers. He is careful not to attribute blame to the monarch herself, but (as in the Grand Remonstrance) to hint darkly at a Popish 'plot'. This, he maintains, will result in 'a most alarming increase in the population of the country', thereby confirming the worst fears of Thomas Malthus, whose influential *Essay on the Principle of Population* (1798; sixth edition 1828) predicted that population growth would outstrip the means of agriculture to sustain mankind, resulting in misery and vice.

It is all good fun. Dickens himself had entered the marital state just under four years previously, and (despite his later jaundiced verdict that the marriage had been disastrous from the start) it is important to recognize that all the evidence of the time indicates that in its early years his relationship with Catherine Hogarth was an extremely happy and harmonious one.[18] *Sketches of Young Couples* resonates with the confidence of a man firmly committed emotionally and intellectually to the sanctity of marriage.

The zest with which the young author contemplates the marital state of the queen spills merrily into *Sketches of Young Couples*. From the outset of Dickens's career comic characterization has been recognized as one of his most

[18] See Michael Slater, *Dickens and Women* (London: Dent, 1983), 133–62, and Lillian Nayder, *The Other Dickens: A Life of Catherine Dickens* (Ithaca, NY: Cornell University Press, 2011).

appealing achievements, and the hallmarks of his approach are abundantly in evidence in these early sketches. The sharp eye for telling detail; the ability to make a character utterly unique even as it is at the same time representative; the knack of introducing surprising comparisons through metaphor and simile; the energetic style which generates such vibrancy, bringing characters swiftly and vividly to life; the range of expression which can move rapidly from ironic detachment to pathos, horror, or fascination—can be seen throughout the volume.

Mr. Merrywinkle is a rather lean and long-necked gentleman, middle-aged and middle-sized, and usually troubled with a cold in the head. Mrs. Merrywinkle is a delicate-looking lady, with very light hair, and is exceedingly subject to the same unpleasant disorder. The venerable Mrs. Chopper—who is strictly entitled to the appellation, her daughter not being very young, otherwise than by courtesy, at the time of her marriage, which was some years ago—is a mysterious old lady who lurks behind a pair of spectacles, and is afflicted with a chronic disease, respecting which she has taken a vast deal of medical advice, and referred to a vast number of medical books, without meeting any definition of the symptoms that at all suits her, or enables her to say, "That's my complaint." Indeed, the absence of authentic information upon the subject of this complaint would seem to be Mrs. Chopper's greatest ill, as in all other respects she is an uncommonly hale and hearty woman. ('The Couple who Coddle themselves')

The suggestive details—Mr Merrywinkle is 'rather lean and long-necked'—the surprising verb—Mrs Chopper 'lurks' behind her spectacles—and the arch observation that the old lady's chief complaint is the lack of a defined complaint—all bring the characters instantly to life. If this is not Dickens at his very best, nevertheless these writings are emphatically better than the cursory disparagement they have too often received—when noticed at all—by modern commentators. Early reviewers were closer to the mark when they praised its '*jeu d'esprit*' (*Literary Gazette*, 15 February 1840), the 'richly wrought description of the different couples' (*Trewman's Exeter Flying Post*, 27 February 1840), containing 'some good hits and some useful hints' (*Essex Standard*, 21 February 1840). And Forster, writing in the *Examiner* (16 February 1840), called it 'a most agreeable and well-timed book. We opened it with a lively recollection of the mirthful Sketches of Young Gentlemen, and found the same racy style, rich humour, and nice expression of character.'

In a recent article (virtually the only scholarly discussion of these sketches) Wendy Parkins assesses *Sketches of Young Couples* as an exploration of 'companionable' homemaking.[19] For more than a decade previously popular melodramas such as J. B. Buckstone's *Luke the Labourer* (1826) and Douglas Jerrold's *Black-Ey'd Susan* (1829) had been celebrating the virtues of domesticity in opposition to Regency raffishness, and the accession of the young queen, following the reigns of the libertine George IV and his brother William IV with his string of illegitimate Fitz-Clarences, was seen at the time to usher in a new spirit of the age, a shift underlined by the royal marriage.[20]

The central unifying ingredient of the three volumes, and one of their chief attractions, is the presence of eighteen

[19] 'Emotions, Ethics and Sociality in Dickens's *Sketches of Young Couples*', *Dickens Quarterly*, 27 (2010), 3–22, at pp. 3–4.
[20] See Paul Schlicke, 'Hazlitt, Horne, and the Spirit of the Age', *SEL Studies in English Literature 1500–1900*, 45 (2005), 829–51, at p. 836.

engravings by Hablot Browne (1815–82), who alone of the originators was identified from the outset by a known pseudonym. As 'Phiz' Browne had previously supplied illustrations and vignette title-page for Dickens's (also pseudonymous) anti-sabbatarian pamphlet *Sunday Under Three Heads* (June 1836), and had immediately thereafter been drafted to supply the illustrations for *Pickwick* when Robert Buss proved an unsatisfactory successor to Robert Seymour. His comic grotesque style, emblematic imagination, and tractable nature made him a congenial collaborator for Dickens, for whom he became principal illustrator in ensuing years, contributing over 700 plates to accompany the novelist's writings.

Phiz worked within the tradition of William Hogarth, James Gillray, Thomas Rowlandson, and the Cruikshanks (Isaac and his sons Isaac Robert and George), in which visual images were presented as emblematic art to be read for meaning. Just as the world about them was for Dickens and Caswall a set of signs to be deciphered, so too the graphic designs offered emblems pregnant with meaning for the viewer to comprehend. The tradition was comic, not only in the sense of laughable, but also in that it was dealing with commonplace subject matter, and satiric, deploying grotesque exaggeration related as much to artistic convention as to caricature of the world represented.[21]

The three cover designs, like the covers of the part-issues of Dickens's later novels, are filled with emblematic details. Thus the one for *Young Ladies* frames the three central figures

---

[21] Ronald Paulson, 'The Tradition of Comic Illustration from Hogarth to Cruikshank', in Robert L. Patten (ed.), *George Cruikshank: A Revaluation* (Princeton: Princeton University Press, 1974), 35–60.

with sewing scissors and thimbles; two lovebirds twined together with a ribbon rest behind the book the ladies inspect, and a Cupid, armed with bow and arrow, peeps over the envelope (sealed with a heart shape) which surmounts the scene. The cover vignette for *Young Gentlemen* depicts two bachelors puffing on a hookah as they lounge insouciantly in the upper half of the page; beneath them one harassed young gentleman kneels, hands over ears, tormented by three young ladies, while opposite him another young gentleman flees in terror from a young lady who restrains him firmly with one hand while holding open an illustrated book with the other. In the cover design for *Young Couples* the young lady in the lower-right corner impales a wedding ring on a lance, while on the right another young lady prepares to wind a heavy chain around the kneeling young gentleman in front of her. Above them to the left a couple are seen from behind approaching the altar, while to their right another young gentleman struggles helplessly to escape the grasp of a young lady. All four couples are encircled by wedding rings, while above them two knowing elves gleefully survey the scene.

Most of the plates which complement the sketches depict symmetrically balanced figures, their placement invariably emblematic of the distribution of power within relationships. The focus of nearly all the engravings is emphatically centralized, giving an impression of calm stability in even the most active scenes. Many groups are surmounted by designs suggestive of a proscenium arch, thereby emphasizing the theatrical nature of the depictions, which look like nothing so much as examples of the tableaux (or, as they were known at the time, 'pictures') with which climactic moments of contemporary stage fare concluded. Exceptions to this poised

and posed quality are the engravings of the Manly Young
Lady, who gallops cheerfully on a horse past an anguished-
looking man as he scrambles to extricate himself from the
puddle into which he has fallen, and the Extremely Natural
Young Lady, who smiles benignly from the comfort of a
chariot at the figure of a forlornly pursuing gentleman (her
bonnet in his hand) while the carriage thunders off the page,
cheered on by amused spectators. Pictures on walls (generally
of paterfamilias and wife), caged birds, boisterous children, a
statuette of Adam and Eve, and other emblems contribute
significantly to the meanings of the engravings.

Accompanied by these delightful illustrations, the sketches
offer a revealing glimpse of courtship rituals and gender
relations at the outset of the Victorian era. They display the
attractiveness of a popular literary mode of the 1830s, and the
contrasts between Caswall's work and Dickens's highlight
the ability of Boz to evoke the distinctiveness of a character
in a few swift strokes. The humour, wit, and exuberance of
these writings afford fascinating evidence of a writer learning
his craft and refining his style, and they constitute a pleasing
complement to Dickens's better-known forays into the mode
of the sketch, in which he excelled throughout his career.

A NOTE ON THE TEXT

Sketches of Young Ladies and *Sketches of Young Gentlemen*
both went through multiple editions as separate volumes
when they first appeared in 1837–8. They were followed in
1840 by *Sketches of Young Couples*, again published as a
single work. *Sketches of Young Ladies* was attributed
pseudonymously to 'Quiz'; authorship of the other two was

not revealed until after Dickens's death in 1870. In 1843 the three titles were gathered into a single volume, and there were further combined editions in 1869 and 1875. The 1869 edition omits 'The Evangelical Young Lady' and the final tribute to the queen; otherwise changes between editions were minimal, consisting primarily in occasional variation in punctuation. The present edition is based on 1869, the final text to appear during Dickens's lifetime, corrected and expanded by comparison with the 1843 and 1875 editions.

ACKNOWLEDGEMENTS

I would like to thank Kim Downie, John Drew, Bill Long, Judith Luna, Judith Napier, Bob Patten, and Michael Slater for their help in preparing this edition.

P.V.W.S

THE SKETCHES

SKETCHES

YOUNG LADIES

BY QUIZ

WITH ILLUSTRATIONS BY PHIZ

Sketches

of

Young Ladies:

IN WHICH THESE INTERESTING MEMBERS OF THE
ANIMAL KINGDOM ARE CLASSIFIED,

ACCORDING TO THEIR SEVERAL

INSTINCTS, HABITS, AND GENERAL
CHARACTERISTICS,

BY "QUIZ."

WITH SIX ILLUSTRATIONS BY

"PHIZ."

ℙREFACE

———·———

𝔚ᴇ have often regretted, that while so much genius has of late years been employed in classifications of the animal and vegetable kingdom, the classification of young ladies has been totally and unaccountably neglected. And yet, who can doubt but that this beautiful portion of the creation exhibits as many, if not more, varieties than any system of botany yet published? Nature, indeed, seems to have exhibited here, more than in any other part of her works, her uncontrollable propensity of ranging at freedom; and, accordingly, has beautifully diversified the female species, not only in respect to their minds and persons, but even in those more important points, their bonnets, gloves, shawls, and other equally interesting portions of dress.

It was in vain that we waited, for more than ten years, in expectation of this philosophical theme being taken up by Cuvier, Dr. Lardner, or Mrs. Somerville. At last, tired of the delay, we determined on trying the subject ourselves, especially as we have always felt a singular pleasure in examining the diversities of the fair sex. There was, however, a difficulty started at the beginning, which seemed wholly insurmountable. How, thought we, are we to find hot-press paper sufficient to contain the characters of every young lady in this island? This consideration detained us two whole calendar months, for six hours a day, with our feet on the fender, our elbows on our knees, and our face in our hands. At last, after intense thought, we came to the conclusion that it might be possible to discover in the youthful fair, certain latent characteristics, under which all the young ladies of this age and country might be classed, without describing each in particular. This idea no sooner struck us, than we sat down at once to our desk; and, allowing ourselves five minutes a-day, and no more, for eating and drinking, paused not till we had completed the whole of the treatise, which is now submitted to the public, and from which we shall no further delay the reader, except to add, that the Linnæan system hath been observed in this classification; all young ladies being Troglodites, and not Ichthyosauri, as Dr. Buckland hath erroneously observed in his late Bridgewater Treatise.

M.P.

CONTENTS

List of Illustrations

ℭHE 𝔜OUNG 𝔏ADY 𝔚HO 𝔖INGS

—◆—

𝔗HOSE who are at all acquainted with society in England must have remarked that in every neighbourhood there is invariably a "young lady who sings." This young lady in general has a voice like that of a tin kettle if it could speak, and takes more pride in reaching as high as D sharp than if she had reached the top of the pyramid of Cheops. Whenever she is invited out, her "mamma" invariably brings four songs by "that dear Mr. Bayly," three German songs, two Italian, and one French song. Sometimes, but not always, an ominous green box is brought in the fly along with the music, enclosing the valuable appendage of a guitar, with a sort of Scotch plaid silk ribbon of no earthly use dangling from the handle.

At tea, if you sit next to the young lady who sings, she is sure to talk about Pasta, and beyond a doubt will ask you if you are fond of music. Beware here of answering in the affirmative. If you do, your fate is sealed for the night; and while half a dozen pretty girls are chatting delightfully together in one corner of the room, as far from the piano as possible, it will be your unhappy destiny to stand at the side of the young lady who sings, turning over the leaves for her, two at once in your confusion. At the conclusion of each song, it will be your particular business to repeat over again the words "most beautiful" three several times; and, while inwardly longing to be flirting with all the six pretty girls in the corner, you will be obliged to beseech and implore the young lady who sings to delight the company with another

9

The Young Lady who Sings

solo. Hereupon the young lady who sings coughs faintly, and says that she has a severe cold; but, much to her private satisfaction, is overruled by her "mamma," who, turning round from the sofa where she is seated, talking scandal with the lady of the house, says reproachfully, "Well, my dear, what if you have a cold—does that prevent you obliging us? For shame!" Then follows a short pantomime between mother and daughter, touching and concerning the next song to be sung. A German song is fixed upon at last, which the daughter goes through in the most pathetic style imaginable, quite ignorant all the time that the subject is a very merry one. All the company pause in their conversation, except the six young ladies in the corner, and the deaf old gentleman who is playing with the poker, on each of whom respectively "mamma" looks scissors. The young lady, having gone right through from beginning to end, stops at last quite out of breath, as might well be expected when it is considered what a race her fingers have had for the last five minutes, in a vain attempt to keep up with her tongue. "How very pretty!" you observe—now that there is room for a word. "I think it is," replies the young lady who sings, in the most simple manner imaginable. "Mamma" now asks successively each of the other mammas whether any of their daughters sing, and, receiving a negative, addresses her daughter thus:—"Julia, love, do you remember that sweet little thing of Madame Stockhausen's, which she sang the other evening?" Hereupon another song follows, and then another at the particular request of the lady of the house, who is all the time dying for her own daughters to exhibit. In this manner the evening is spent; and, if you are particularly fortunate, you have, in return for your patient listening, the exquisite gratification of putting on the young lady's shawl, before she steps into the fly, in which she hums all the way home.

We have been a considerable frequenter of parties in our time, and never went to one but the pleasure of it was interrupted more or less by the appearance of the young lady who sings. At last, on this very account we gave up going to parties altogether, till one day we had an invitation to a very pleasant house, and received at the same time from another quarter authentic information that the young lady who sings was gone into Wales. This news led us to accept the invitation at once. "At last," thought we, "we shall enjoy an evening in peace." We went. Coffee came in, and there was no sign of our enemy. Our heart leapt with delight, and we were just beginning to enjoy a philosophical conversation on raspberry-jam with the matter-of-fact young lady, when to our complete consternation, in walked the guitar, the young lady who sings, and her eternal "mamma," all three evidently bent on destruction. It appears that the young lady, hearing of the party, had kindly put off her departure for Wales just one day, on purpose to be present.

We can say nothing as to what followed this hostile incursion, for having been unhappily fated to the possession of a tolerable ear, we were obliged to beat a retreat at once. Since that memorable occasion we have never gone to any party whatever, without first ascertaining, beyond a possibility of doubt, that the young lady who sings is not to be one of the number.

𝕿HE 𝕭USY 𝖄OUNG 𝕷ADY

𝖂E used to suppose, in our more juvenile days, that there was but one "busy young lady" in the world; for at that time no more than one of this large class had come under our philosophic cognisance. This young lady was eternally occupied from morning till night in doing something or other, but what that was we could never discover, either for love or money. We confess that, to our simple judgement, it sometimes appeared that she was never doing anything at all. But how could this be, when she used to assure everybody, a dozen times every day, that she was the busiest person in the world?

Among all her multifarious occupations, there was one at which she laboured with assiduity unequalled since the days of Penelope. This consisted in sitting before the fire in front of a wooden machine like a pillory, across which was drawn a very tight piece of canvas. On this canvas, with patience unparalleled, and energies that never gave way, she would work for hours in the production of a green worsted cat, with yellow eyes and vermilion tail. Somehow or other, however, it is matter of historical fact, that she never got beyond the beginning of the tail and the tip of the left ear. Either her worsted was not to be found when she wanted to re-thread her needle; or somebody came in; or somebody went out; or she was called imperiously away to some other business of still greater importance, such as to water the new geranium; or to write out a piece of music which she never finished; or to

13

take a ribbon off her bonnet; or to put it on again; or to change her shoes for a walk, which always ended in her changing her mind and not walking. It was not to be supposed that a young lady with so many occupations of her own making could find time for writing letters. Accordingly her epistles, unlike the epistles of young ladies in general, were for the most part very short and sprawly, and always broke up abruptly thus:— "Really, my dear, you can't think how busy I am just now. I have *so* much to do. We all unite," &c. &c.

It would be thought that, with all this business, our young lady would find some necessity for keeping her multitudinous concerns in some sort of manageable order. No such thing. Even our juvenile recollection enables us to make an affidavit, if necessary, that her little rosewood workbox, so prettily lined with blue silk, was sufficiently unarranged inside to gratify the most inordinate lover of nature's irregularities. The thimble and scissors were everlastingly involved in a labyrinth of fancy-coloured German wools. Did you wish to find a needle, you had a longer voyage of discovery to make than Columbus himself. A piece of unentangled thread was out of the question. There were so many pieces of fashionable work, begun but never completed, lying higgledy-piggledy in that same workbox, that it might fairly be called the burial-place of fancy works cut off in their infancy. Let it not be supposed, however, that fancy alone was allowed to preside there. More than once, in the prying days of our youth, we have beheld, peeping out from under the lid, the toe end of a half-darned stocking, agreeably diversified with the unfinished fringe of an unwashed night-cap. Not to speak of all those unhappy gloves, belonging to young gentlemen, which the busy young lady had no sooner got hold of, promising to mend (a favourite practice of hers), than they might be considered as laid up in limbo for life; nor of the little pink memorandum-book, which seemed to have an inborn predisposition of protruding itself to view, whenever there was a secret of unusual importance committed to it.

As we have observed before, we used in former times to consider this busy young lady as the only one of her class. By degrees, however, as we have enlarged our knowledge of things, we have discovered that she is only a type of a thousand others. There are now, within the range of our acquaintance, no less than five fine specimens. Two of them are sisters, and, in a zoological point of view, may be considered the noblest pair yet discovered of those useful animals that practise the happy art of doing everything and nothing at the same time.

The Romantic Young Lady

———•———

THERE is at present existing in a plain brick house, within twenty miles of our habitation, a young lady whom we have christened "the romantic young lady" ever since she came to an age of discretion. We have known her from her childhood, and can safely affirm that she did not take this turn till her fifteenth year, just after she had read Corinne, which at that time was going the round of the reading society.

At that period she lived with her father in the next village. We well remember calling accidentally, and being informed by her that it was "a most angelic day," a truth which certainly our own experience of the cold and wet in walking across would have inclined us to dispute. These were the first words which gave us a hint as to the real state of the young lady's mind; and we know not but we might have passed them over, had it not been for certain other expressions on her part, which served as a confirmation of our melancholy suspicions. Thus, when our attention was pointed at a small sampler, lying on the table, covered over with three alphabets in red, blue, and black, with a miniature green pyramid at the top, she observed pathetically that "it was done by herself in her *infancy*;" after which, turning to a dandelion in a wine-glass, she asked us languishingly if we loved flowers, affirming in the same breath that "she quite doted on them, and verily believed that if there were no flowers she should die outright." These expressions caused us a lengthened meditation on the young lady's case, as we walked home over the fields. Nor, with all allowances made, could we avoid the melancholy conclusion that she was gone romantic. "There is no hope for her," said we to ourselves. "Had she only gone mad, there might have been some chance." As usual, we were correct in our surmises. Within two months after this, our romantic friend ran away with the hairdresser's apprentice, who settled her in the identical plain brick house so honourably mentioned above.

From our observations upon this case, and others of a similar kind, we feel no hesitation in laying before our readers the following characteristics, by which they shall know a romantic young lady within the first ten minutes of introduction. In the first place, you will observe that she always drawls more or less, using generally the drawl pathetic, occasionally diversified with the drawls sympathetic, melancholic, and semi-melancholic. Then she is always pitying or wondering. Her pity knows no bounds. She pities "the poor flowers in winter." She pities her friend's shawl if it gets wet. She pities poor Mr. Brown, "he has such a taste; nothing but cabbages and potatoes in his garden." 'Tis singular that, with all this fund of compassion, she was never known to pity a deserving object. That would be too much matter of fact. Her compassion is of a more ætherial texture. She never gave a halfpenny to a beggar, unless he was "an exceedingly picturesque young man." Next to the passion of pity, she is blest with that of love. She loves the moon. She loves each of the stars individually. She loves the sea, and when she is out in a small boat loves a storm of all things. Her dislikes, it must be confessed, are equally strong and capacious. Thus she hates that dull woman, Mrs. Briggs. She can't bear that dry book, Rollin's History. She detests high roads. Nothing with her is in the mean. She either dotes or abominates. If you dance with her at a ball, she is sure to begin philosophising, in a small way, about the feelings. She is particularly partial to wearing fresh flowers in her hair at dinner. You would be perfectly thunderstruck to hear, from her own lips, what an immense number of dear friends she has, both young and old, male and female. Her correspondence with young ladies is something quite appalling. She was never known, however, in her life, to give one piece of actual information, except in a postscript. Her handwriting is excessively Lilliputian, yet she always crosses in red ink, and sometimes recrosses again in invisible green. She has read all the love novels in Christendom, and is quite in love with that dear Mr. Bulwer. Some prying persons say that she has got the complete works of Lord Byron; but on that point no one is perfectly certain. If she has a younger brother fresh from school, he is always ridiculing her for what she says, trying to put her in a passion, in which, however, he rarely succeeds. There is one thing in which she excels half her sex, for she hates scandal and gossip.

To conclude, the naturalist may lay down three principal eras in the romantic young lady's life:—the first from fifteen to nineteen, while she is growing romantic; the second from nineteen to twenty-one, while she keeps romantic; and the third from twenty-one to twenty-nine, during which time she gradually subsides into common sense.

ᙢHE ᙚVANGELICAL ᙥOUNG ᙢADY

Far be it from us to decry true religion wherever it be found, more especially among the youthful fair, who can wear no ornament more precious or becoming. But of late there has sprung up a strange sort of morbid religion among the young ladies of our neighbourhood, which deserves especial notice; since it is to this that we attribute the reduction of our county balls from four a year to one; the total abolition of our archery meeting, and the insolvency of the dancing-master, who lives in the next town.

We carefully watched the whole progress of this disease in destroying the innocent mirth of our neighbourhood, and can affirm most indubitably on the strictest historical evidence, that it began with Miss Slugs, the attorney's daughter, about a year-and-a-half ago. That distance of time has now elapsed since upon paying a visit in that quarter, we found the once cheerful and vivacious Miss Slugs, sitting in the drawing-room in a very plain dress, with an extremely sulky look, and doing nothing. We began our conversation with her in our usual mirthful style, which she had been accustomed to approve of. But to each of our several witticisms she replied with only a cool yes or no. At last, fancying that we had hit on something to please her, we asked whether she was going to the ball on Friday. What was our surprise when, starting back in the utmost horror, Miss Slugs answered in this manner—"I thought," said she, "you were aware that I never go to balls now. I consider them to be extremely improper." After this she gratuitously quoted for our exclusive information two or three passages of Scripture, to all which we listened reverently, as we always do when Scripture is read, yet not without pain at thinking how greatly she perverted those doctrines, which, however serious in their ultimate object, are yet in our humble opinion by no means opposed to occasional mirth.

We did not again visit Miss Slugs for some time; but every now and then reports reached us that she was becoming daily more particular. First we heard that she had prevailed on her mother to dress the two maid-servants in plain uniform of blue and white. Then came the report that she had set up a private Sunday school in opposition to the parish minister. By degrees she did not come to church so often as usual, leaving her mother to come alone. This surprised us particularly. We are curious, if not inquisitive. We called on our neighbours, inquiring the cause of this dereliction on the part of Miss Slugs. It appeared that in her opinion our minister, who is a very excellent man, and a great friend of

The Evangelical Young Lady

the Bishop's, did not preach the Gospel. We puzzled ourselves to discover what she could be at during church time, since she did not come to church. But the task was beyond us. A faint rumour, and nothing more, reached us that on such occasions she sat before the kitchen fire with the cook-maid, reading tracts. Accounts now spread of various small quarrels between Mrs. Slugs and Miss Slugs on the subject of religion. It seems the old lady could not be prevailed on to forswear a pink ribbon in her cap. Anything else she was willing to give up to please her daughter, but not the pink ribbon. The pink ribbon, therefore, was a perpetual source of dispute, which did not end till the daughter herself cut it off one night when her mother was in bed. This news, important as it was, hardly prepared us for the next step of Miss Slugs, which was no less than a secession from the Established Church. At first we doubted our ears—but the report gained ground, and there was no course but to believe it. All doubt was finally removed from our mind two or three weeks after by the witness of our own eyes; for as we were walking on a Sunday morning along the banks of a small river, we came upon a shady place where about two hundred persons were collected, all looking very intently upon the centre of the stream. We ourselves turned our eyes in the same direction, and beheld the anabaptist blacksmith and carpenter in the very act of turning Miss Slugs backwards into the water. She was dressed in flannel for the occasion. The case was plain. Miss Slugs had become an anabaptist, and the next day—married the carpenter.

Although no other young ladies followed the example of Miss Slugs to the extent which she went, there was scarce one, saving and except the romantic and matter-of-fact young ladies, who was not touched with a spirit of secession more or less. With some the fit lasted a fortnight. With others three or four months. With a few half a year. During this time, the balls were attended by old maids only, and in consequence received great detriment, from which they have not yet recovered. At present, the young ladies are pretty nearly come back to their senses. It is only to be hoped that they will not become as violently fond of amusements, as they have lately been violently opposed to them. This sudden change is often the case in republics, and perhaps even the republic of young ladies is not exempt from a liability to such an extravagance. In our humble opinion, to go to a ball three or four times in the year is both a rational and cheerful amusement for the young of both sexes. But it is better to become an anabaptist at once, like Miss Slugs, than, like some ladies whom I know, to waste heart, health, and energy, in a continual pursuit of irreclaimable frivolity.

THE MATTER-OF-FACT YOUNG LADY

—•—

OPPOSED to the romantic young lady, a class daily becoming smaller, there is a class very common in these utilitarian times, whom we designate "the matter-of-fact young ladies," for want of a better name. These young ladies are always most particularly cautious in everything connected with them and theirs. They were never known to receive a kiss from their male cousins, are always most punctiliously neat, and anticipate old maidenism by ten years, being scrupulous beyond measure in wearing dresses as plain and angular as themselves. Their conversation is wholly on actual things, without the slightest intrusion of an idea. They take literally everything that you say, and are never surprised by anything. You will not find a book of poetry on their shelves. The first row will, beyond doubt, be nothing but dictionaries; the second, abridgments of histories and recipes. In general they have no ear for music, and never touched a piano in their life. There are a variety of things of which they could never see the use. Thus they could never see the use of drawing, when prints can be had so cheap. They could never see the use of fancy work. They could never see the use of dancing.

We once met one of these matter-of-fact young ladies, in company with the romantic young lady. Nothing could be more amusing than the contrast. Whatever put the romantic young lady into ecstasies was sure to make the matter-of-fact young lady look more than usually dull and insipid. When the romantic young lady expressed her intense delight at the beauty of the evening, the matter-of-fact young lady averred that she could see nothing in the night more than common, except that it was very likely to give a cold.

But, to proceed with the characteristics which we were giving, it is to be observed that your matter-of-fact young ladies, if you are admitted suddenly into the sitting-room, will invariably be found engaged in the delightful process of mending a stocking. Your entrance, you would suppose, might interrupt this delicate work. By no means. The matter-of-fact young lady sees nothing in it, as some others of our weaker-minded acquaintance might; but goes on as unconcernedly as ever, till the heel is finished off in regular rows of parallel straight lines, like a miniature ploughed field. Every now and then, without lifting up her eye, she gives you a word, which you answer. Her first question is invariably concerning the health of your paternal ancestor, her second ditto about your mother, her third ditto about your sister Mary Anne, and so on through the catalogue. She then hopes that you yourself are in good health, and having declined the word health from beginning to end, asks confidentially, who it is that mends *your* stockings, thus making a gentle reference to her own pleasing occupation. After this she tells you, without asking, to your eternal satisfaction, that her brother John went out shooting yesterday with a gun, and killed two sparrows; that her father is gone into the town about old Betty's leg, which she broke three weeks ago, in getting over the stile near Mrs. Smith's; and that her mother is in the kitchen, watching the cook making raspberry jam. This leads her to various acute observations, first on jam in general, and secondly on raspberry jam in particular. She asks you how your mother makes it; and, having thus amused you as much as she thinks proper for some twenty minutes, informs you graciously that she must be going now, since she "is wanted." You make your bow and exit together, saying inwardly, "Hang her, for a matter-of-fact young lady!"

THE PLAIN YOUNG LADY

———•———

IN every tolerable neighbourhood there are sure to be found four or five specimens of "the plain young lady;" by which term we do not simply understand a mere want of beauty, but also the actual appropriation and possession, more or less, of red hair, goggle eyes, black teeth, small-pox, beard, and other agreeable et ceteras, all of which together give to some of our young ladies a touching appearance not easily forgot.

One of the most striking characteristics of the plain young lady is her ignorance of dress. Whether she thinks herself too ugly to be improved anyhow, we know not; but certain it is, that she exhibits a most melancholy want of taste in this particular, always fixing on those especial colours which most exhibit the badness of her complexion. Then, again, in respect to the fit, she is seldom so particular as we could desire. She has never been known to send the same dress back to be altered more than five times running. When, however, we have brought these charges against the plain young lady, we have brought all. In every other respect she is generally to be admired. Almost all the plain young ladies, whom we have the pleasure of knowing, have got sweet voices, and many of them are blest with a very good figure. Then they are sensible, in the long-run; sketch to perfection, and work like the very patron saint of sempstresses. In respect to this last particular we do not hesitate to say, that if two young ladies, one pretty and the other plain, were to oblige us by an offer of making a shirt-collar, we would instantly fix on the plain young lady. Moreover, the plain young lady is generally amiable, a great beauty in young ladies, for the want of which no other perfection can compensate. Never having been flattered, she has no affectation; and if you observe her narrowly, you will find that she has picked up a great deal of useful knowledge one way or another.

For our own part, we do not blush to own that of late we have acquired a particular preference for plain young ladies. Time was, indeed, when, with the rest of our sex, we thought lightly of them; but of this prejudice we were cured some months back, in the following manner:—We had been told that a most particularly plain young lady was to be present at a small party to which we had been invited. This was told us in confidence, but so late as to prevent our sending an excuse. We prepared accordingly for the party with ominous forebodings; neglecting our usual accuracy in the tie of our stock, and the evenness of our silk stockings. The very first person to whom we were introduced was the plain young lady; and we found her to be still plainer than we had imagined. Fortune placed her next us at dinner. What could we do? We must be civil. Accordingly we hazarded three words of observation on the weather. The plain young lady replied; we were struck with her voice. She asked us a question which we could not answer; we discovered her to be clever. She went on, and we found that she was amiable. What remained but that in five minutes more we forgot that she was plain altogether! and have never been persuaded of it since. At tea we again sat next to the plain young lady, and were fast falling in love with her, when a friend whispered that she was engaged to the handsomest man in the neighbourhood.

From that time we have admired plain young ladies, and humbly request every other gentleman to follow our example—if he is able.

THE LITERARY YOUNG LADY

IF there is one young lady whom we should be more afraid of leading to the hymeneal altar than another, it is the literary young lady; by which term we do not simply understand the young lady who takes in the Scientific Magazine, but her whose whole life and thoughts are so mixed up with literature, that she cannot for the world bring out a single consecutive sentence without touching on the state of letters here and abroad. What disgusts us most with the literary young lady, is the fact that she is invariably most particularly ignorant of everything, and of nothing more than of her own ignorance.

The other day we called upon a young lady of this class, and the first words which she uttered were the following:— "Oh, Mr. P——, have you seen the new magazine—what's its name? You should see it. It's so cleverly conducted. I know it will please you." To this interrogation we answered in the negative, and were proceeding to inquire pathetically concerning the health of the literary young lady's grandmother, when she interrupted us by asking us seriously, upon our honour, how far Poltzikouski had got in his grand Russian dictionary. "Oh, Mr. P——," said she, "what a splendid work that will be when it's finished! I am so anxious. Only think! twelve cubic feet of knowledge, genuine Russian knowledge, all in a lump! Then there's the Pickwick for this month. Have you seen it, Mr. P——? Dear delightful Mr. Pickwick, how I love him!" Hereupon the literary young lady started at a tangent, without warning, into another room, which she calls

27

her study, and within five seconds, came back with a small book, which she set before us, saying it was Spanish, and begging us to explain a sentence which she could not make out. "Only think," said she, "I began Spanish last Tuesday week, and am now at page 180 of Don Quixote. How I love that old Don Quixote! and it sounds so much better in Spanish too." Upon this the literary young lady commenced reading Spanish with such a pronunciation as would have caused us to run out of the room, if we had not been on the look-out for some luncheon. When she had got through a page to her no small satisfaction, she paused suddenly, and addressed us as follows:—"Now, Mr. P——, I've got you, and you shan't escape. Don't you remember that you promised to write down for me, in this album, one of your poetical effusions? Sit down, there's a good man. Here's the pen and everything. You need not fill more than four pages, but mind you write clear." Thus were we, half ravenous with hunger, forced to sit down and write for one mortal hour with no redress, half of which time the literary young lady was looking over our shoulder to see how we got on, and the other half translating a French divine into her best English, and a square red book. When we had concluded our performance, we thought we were released, and were preparing to depart to the pastry-cook's, when the literary young lady compelled us to sit down and hear her criticisms upon Milton's verses, which we had just been writing from memory, but which in her simple mind she thought to be our own composition. She then informed us, gratuitously, that a most scientific work had been just published by Murray, with which we could not fail of being highly delighted. "But," said she, "mind you read it with attention. It is so very deep. I assure you I took all yesterday morning in getting through the first half. It's all about steam-engines, stars, hieroglyphics, and that sort of thing, you know. Highly interesting, I assure you. But I don't exactly agree with the author in what he says about steam-engines going by gas." This led to a long discussion on the state of science all over the world, and in that town in particular; and we verily believe we should have been compelled to stay till this moment, talking about Franks, Ariosto, and craniology, had it not been for the fortunate entrance of the literary young lady's mother, who asked her angrily how she had forgotten to order dinner; whereto the literary young lady replied with dignity, that she could not always be thinking of such trivial matters. Hereupon "mamma" flew into a rage, and was just going to box the young lady's literary ear, when we made our escape.

The whole class of literary young ladies may be easily distinguished by their resemblance to our fair friend; but we shall add the following characteristics, that there may be no mistake. In the first place, if she does not esteem it too unintellectual to attend a ball, she always shows her contempt for it by wearing soiled kid gloves. Then, it is ten to one but she is radically inclined, and calls you mister. She scarce ever walks out except to the bookseller's, with whose young man she converses on the most easy terms imaginable, asking whether such a book has come out yet, and, if it has, what he thinks of it. In the circulating library she is well known, but only reads the scientific books. If she live in a town (as she does in nine cases out of ten), she is sure to know the writer of that very singular paragraph in last week's paper, but won't tell, ask her ever so much: that would never do! We have never yet had positive evidence of the literary young lady writing in poet's corner. In general she is above poetry, preferring history, philosophy, steam, and the fine arts. But yet we cannot help fancying that, in our paper of this week, some "Stanzas," entitled "Love's a Dream," are by our literary friend. They are so dry, and so borrowed. Then, again, the literary young lady is sure to have a collection of handwritings, and three or four old halfpence, which she calls her coins, and piously kisses one by one every time she opens the box, telling you that they belonged to one of the Neros, or so. Of late she has taken to political economy and geology, and tells you very profoundly that she highly approves of Cuvier.

Thus much for positive characteristics, two or three of which, if you find together in any young lady, set her down at once as an aspirant to old maidenism—in other words, as a literary young lady. For if it be true, as I have observed in society, that some young ladies become old maids sooner and others later, certainly it is that the literary young lady outstrips all others in the race, and often becomes a confirmed old maid at the age of three-and-twenty, when her elders are still in their youth.

The Manly Young Lady

———•———

There is a sort of young lady rarely met with in these times, whom we call "the manly young lady." This specimen is found most in those counties where there is good hunting, and prefers the north to the south. There is one at present quite perfect within a hundred miles of Cambridge, and two-and-twenty years old, to use her own expression.

The manly young lady talks a great deal of dogs and horses, distinguishing them by their sex. Thus she feels no repugnance whatever in signifying to you her favourite female dog by a short monosyllable, and always says, "My mare." She always makes her calls on horseback, dressed in an old blue riding-habit, none the better for wear, with a little ground-ash in her hand, which she has a knack of flourishing about all the time she is speaking. She is generally seen with her father, the squire, a stout thick gentleman in tops. She was never known to work with a needle, but is a capital hand at netting with a large mesh for the fruit trees. Once, indeed, she attempted to hem a pocket-handkerchief, but after two weeks' labour desisted in the middle of the work. Her shoes are always very thick at the sole; none of your weak flimsy ladies' shoes, but regular solids, and no mistake; made by John Cummings, the village manufacturer and post-office keeper, under her own express direction.

The manly young lady always wished to be a boy, ever since she was a child in arms. In conversation, she is most particularly positive; and should you sit next her at dinner, ten to one but she puts you down half a dozen times at least. If you do not ask her to take wine before the fish is removed, she is sure to ask you herself, making you blush, and looking all the time as unconcerned as if she were your father. Mind that on these occasions you fill her glass to the brim, if you wish to escape further confusion. Should you help her, as you do other ladies, no more than half-full, she will not stickle at it, but will tell you at once that you don't half please her. One thing be most particularly cautious of, and that is, never to

The Manly Young Lady

dine at the same table with her after you have been hunting in her company. She will be sure to entertain the party with some anecdote at your expense. Although our acquaintance is very extensive, we have known intimately but one manly young lady in our time, and of her we always felt afraid. It was quite wonderful how she would tell an anecdote making against our reputation as a horseman. Such bangers she would introduce for the sake of giving her stories a zest, that we felt half inclined to challenge her to mortal combat, forgetting altogether that she was a woman.

The favourite accomplishments of the manly young lady are whistling and playing the flute. In general she changes with the barometer, which she has had hung up by a nail in her own bedroom for her own exclusive use. In fine weather, when she can get out, she is all spirits; in wet weather she sits moping in doors, looking over the Sporting Magazine, or reading Isaak Walton. She was never yet seen by naturalists in the act of reading a novel; and as for love stories, abhors them as trash. She is always certain of a pretty property, so what need is there that she should be falling in love? especially when she is so well able to take care of herself, that she has been known to travel alone, outside the coach, all the way from Manchester to London. We do not hesitate to affirm this, because we are certain that we ourselves once met her. It was about eleven at night, and our coach had stopped to take supper. We ourselves had been sitting inside to be out of the wind. We alighted, and, after two or three minutes' delay in looking after our trunk and bag, walked into the supper room. What was our surprise, to behold a young lady sitting at the head of the table, surrounded by strange gentlemen, and pouring out the tea, in the coolest manner imaginable, just as if the strange gentlemen were her own brothers. This, thought we, must be the manly young lady; and so it was, sure enough, as we soon discovered from her conversation, which turned entirely on the nature of the new patent drag.

Whether these sort of accomplishments are admired by the poor, we know not; but certain it is that the manly young lady is invariably beloved by her humble village neighbours. It might be thought that the true reason of this is a mutual vulgarity. But here we beg to state most positively, for once and all, that, however vulgar may be what the manly young lady does, yet she has a way of doing it, and a sort of natural stylishness about her, which precludes the possibility of any one imagining her to be otherwise than a perfect lady in all points. This, indeed, might be expected from her birth; for it is an invariable rule, that the manly young lady has good connections, and a baronet for her uncle at least, if not for her father. The true cause of her popularity with the poor we take to be this, that she has not got an atom of pride about her, but is both willing and able to talk with them familiarly on their concerns. She knows the proper age for killing a pig, and the best food for fattening him; gives good advice about planting potatoes; finds a buyer for the calf; and calls all the children by their Christian names, without confusing Jim with Jack.

We confess, to our shame, that, being of a retiring disposition, we had always held in abhorrence the manly young lady whom we have before mentioned as our acquaintance. She frightened us; and we, in turn, took every opportunity of avoiding both her and her anecdotes. One cold frosty morning, however, we were perfectly cured of our animosity, by meeting her walking through the snow, and carrying in her own hand a basin of broth for sick Betty Gore.

Since then, we have always felt an interest for her, and were quite rejoiced when, a year afterwards, she married a young clergyman, and settled down all at once into the most domestic and useful of wives that we ever had the pleasure of numbering among our acquaintance.

THE YOUNG LADY WHO IS ENGAGED

SOME of our readers may be surprised that we consider the fact of an engagement as sufficient to establish a young lady under an entirely new head of classification. But those who, like ourselves, are acquainted with the fair sex in a philosophical manner, must be well aware that, no sooner is a young lady engaged, than the very next second she is an altered being. We might almost say that she ceases to preserve her identity; for, by this simple process, we have known the romantic young lady become sensible, the busy young lady become diligent, and the matter-of-fact young lady become romantic.

It is to no purpose that we have philosophised and re-philosophised upon the cause of this sudden change. Sometimes we have thought that all young ladies, without exception, must be hypocrites, and intentionally deceive the world in respect to their true characters, until they become engaged. But this hypothesis we were compelled to give up as incompatible with the acknowledged amiability of the fair sex. Then we conceived the possibility of every young lady leading a sort of chrysalis life, and altering, by a particular

35

regulation of nature, into various forms of character according to the various eras of young-lady life. Thus, before she comes out, she is a mere chrysalis; after she comes out, a gay butterfly; and when she is engaged, a sober moth. But even this position was untenable, when we considered, that whereas the butterfly undergoes fixed changes, the changes of young ladies are altogether without regularity, and cannot be counted upon as anything certain. Other hypotheses we attempted, but none would explain the difficulty; so at last we relinquished the attempt for some future philosopher.

But, to return from this digression, we now proceed to show how you may satisfy yourself that a young lady is engaged or not.

First, then, there will always be a very strong report of it, one-third of which you may fairly believe, especially if your sisters have heard it from the ladies'-maid while she was "doing" their hair. When you have fully and philosophically established in your mind what quantum of belief the report deserves, you may proceed to work, without delay, by paying a visit boldly at the house where lives the young lady herself. When you knock, mind that you knock softly. "Is any one at home?" you ask of John as he opens the door. "Only Miss Higgins, sir," says John, with a knowing side-wink of the eye, not meant, of course, for you to see. The next moment you are shown slap into the drawing-room, and there find Miss Higgins and Mr. Brown sitting opposite one another at each side of the fire. Here an unphilosophical intellect would jump at once to the conclusion that the report of their engagement is correct. I trust that your mind is too logical to be so hasty. At a single glance, like a great general, you mark their position, particularly observing whether the chairs appear to have been hurriedly separated at your approach. These observations I shall suppose you to make while walking from the door up to the fire-place. It depends now entirely on your own management whether your future manœuvres shall advance you a step in your line of evidence. Much, of course, must be left to circumstances, and much to your own peculiar genius. Some persons, of a coarse intellect, would cry out at once "Hallo! what's here?" and observe the degree of blushing on either side consequent upon such an exclamation. Of course, if you are vulgar, you will pursue this course; but if you are a gentleman, as, for this book's sake, I hope you are, you will merely gently insinuate various observations bearing on the matter in hand, remarking particularly what ocular telegraphs pass between them all the while. Thus you come to the conclusion that there is a strong probability the parties are engaged. If the gentleman obstinately sit you out, of course that goes down as additional evidence.

Some persons might here rest satisfied with their discoveries—but you, I trust, have too much laudable curiosity in your nature, and too philosophical a turn of mind, to be satisfied with anything short of a categorical conclusion. You do not want to settle the hypothetical probability of the young lady being engaged; but whether at this present time she be actually, affirmatively, *bonâ fide* engaged. Accordingly, keeping in your mind's eye every link of the chain of evidence already laid before you, you no sooner meet the gentleman some day by accident in the street, than, putting on the most friendly tone imaginable, you shake him a dozen times by the hand, saying affectionately, "My dear fellow, I congratulate you heartily; from my soul I do. What a lucky man you are!" Hereupon, if your friend or acquaintance protest that he can't understand you, with a sort of falter in his voice, and semi-smile struggling at each corner of his mouth, set him down as trying to deceive you. These signs you add to your former presumptive evidence, and so come at last to the conclusion that the young lady is engaged. Others may have reached the same point long before, but you alone have the conscientious feeling of having satisfied your praise-worthy curiosity, by gradual and certain steps, through a regular process of logical deduction.

We shall now give you for your help, in case you may still be at a loss, the following characteristics of the young lady who is engaged:—

In the first place you will observe that the other young ladies invariably make way every day for the same gentleman at her side, after which effort they will probably retire in a compact body to the furthest end of the room, and begin whispering. Then "papa" and "mamma" are always more deferential to her than common; and every now and then at a party "mamma" may be observed looking anxiously about for her; on each of which several occasions a young gentleman comes up and sits by "mamma" for some two minutes and three-quarters, talking confidentially on some subject unknown. The young lady herself, if before this she was particularly shy of yourself and other young gentlemen, now talks to you all in the most sisterly and easy manner possible. But this is only when the "gentleman" is away,—when he is present she only answers "Yes" or "No" to whatever interrogation you may put. Then, again, mark the walk of the engaged young lady. Observe how matrimonial it is. None of your hop-steps-and-jumps, as it used to be, but a staid, sober pace, fit for Lady Macbeth. Even her dress alters and shifts itself to suit her new condition by a sort of automaton effort. Instead of fine French muslin, she is now content with the cheapest poplin. If you drop in early you are sure to find a handsome night-cap, half made, lying on the table under a heap of books hastily thrown over. The young lady herself, wonderful to say, has taken to accounts; and her "mamma" makes her spend half an hour or so every day in the kitchen, to learn pastry matters. Nothing more is wanting as a final confirmation of the surmises which these appearances tend to produce, than to meet the pair out walking together at some unusual time in some unusual place. This you will be sure to succeed in if you take the trouble; and however much others may be surprised some fine morning by the present of a small triangular piece of bride-cake, you yourself will not be surprised in the least, but will go on with your muffin, just remarking by the way to your mother, "that you knew it all long ago."

THE STUPID YOUNG LADY

THE stupid young lady comprises, to speak the truth, by no means a small class of the fair sex. Every one has met, in his time, with a specimen. It is generally very short, very fat, and very amiable. It always has a younger sister who surpasses it in everything but good-nature. Although it began music two years before the younger sister, it was overtaken in two years and three months, do what it would. The same with dancing, French, drawing, Italian, and geography. Although in each of these severally "mamma" gave the stupid young lady a fair start, its younger sister invariably passed it by, before the stupid young lady could look round. And yet, it is very odd, but somehow or other the stupid young lady never showed any anger at this act of rebellion. Nay, if truth must be told, it is even hinted that more than once the stupid young lady has taken advantage of it, by claiming her younger sister's assistance when she was oppressed with the burden of a harder French exercise than usual.

There is a beautifully simple and philosophic expression ever in the stupid young lady's mouth, comprised in the three touching words, "I don't know." These three words are a perfect talisman in her hands for getting her out of any difficulty, however great it may seem. "In what part of England is Liverpool?" asks "mamma." "I don't know," says the stupid young lady. "Who was Alexander?" "I don't know," says the stupid young lady. "In what period of the world did Abraham live?" "I don't know," says the stupid young lady, "but I should think—" "What do you think, love?" says mamma encouragingly. "I should think in the dark ages, mamma."

Such are the sort of answers which the stupid young lady gives to "mamma," or the governess. But the most amusing thing of all, is to see her studying Rollin alone. The other day we had the good fortune to be shown into the drawing-room, while the stupid young lady was sitting before the fire engaged in this very task. We shall never forget her appearance. There she sate on a low stool, looking so fat, so stupid, and so amiable, that we half burst out laughing. "I'm reading Rollin," said the stupid young lady, without rising. "It's very hard. All about Macedonians, Greeks, Turks, and heretics.

I can't understand one word." "I dare say not," said we. The stupid young lady sighed from the bottom of her heart, like the plaintive grunt of a sleeping pig. "What can be the use of reading at all, Mr. P——? Mamma says that it is very profitable, but I am sure I don't think so." Hereupon the stupid young lady fell half-asleep, and dropped her Rollin inside the fender. We picked it up, as in duty bound, and presented it to her. "I don't want it," said the stupid young lady.

Whether her stupidity be the cause, we know not, but certain it is that the stupid young lady always has an extremely happy face. She is quite the picture of health and contentment. Nothing can put her out. Nothing can alter her spirits, which go as uniform as a patent chronometer. Whenever there is any easy tedious work to be done, it is always passed over to her as a matter of course. I will vouch that she darns all her brother's stockings. She is always willing to oblige where she can, and is both liked better and teased more than any other member of the family. We have been quite delighted at seeing her playing a duet with her younger sister, in which, although she has the secondo, she is constantly making a world of blunders, and is as constantly rebuked by her mother, and frowned on by her sister. She tries again and again, but with no better success. The two sisters invariably get out before they have played twenty bars. "Mamma" gets in a passion, and calls her a "stupid thing." "I know I am," says she. Ditto, says her sister; ditto reply. At last both sister and mother look quite perplexed and pained. Intense grief is on the face of each, especially if the duet be before company. Turn for a moment from the face of these two, to the face of the stupid young lady, the guilty cause of all this anxiety. Absolutely there she sits without a single ruffle disturbing her broad, fat, contented face. "How very amiable!" whispers one of the company. "What a delightful temper!" says a second. "I declare I like that stupid Miss Brown," says a third as she is going home in the carriage. "She is so good-natured. It's quite ridiculous."

THE INTERESTING YOUNG LADY

———

WHOEVER is at all in the habit of going to evening parties, must have frequently observed, sitting on the sofa by the fire-side, with an air of the most profound melancholy, the interesting young lady. She is generally jammed in between two fat old ladies, who talk across her, but in whose conversation she never bears a part. Her face is unusually long; something between tallow and spermaceti in complexion. A long corkscrew ringlet dangles down at each side, round which she occasionally twists her fore-finger in a solemn melodramatic style. Evidently her thoughts are "far away." She never utters a syllable to any one. Now and then she wrinkles her forehead just to denote the intense misery that is passing within. Her posture, so far as can be contrived between two fat old ladies, is essentially picturesque; her head thrown back in a delightfully negligent manner; her eyes turned up to the ceiling; her legs crossed, with the toe slanting downwards, as straight as a ruler, and one of her hands thrown carelessly on her lap, upside down.

The Interesting Young Lady

At each introduction, she bows in the most elegant style imaginable. A gracious smile lights up her features for a moment; after which she relapses into her former unconscious state of profound thoughtfulness. Blue, diversified with white, is her constant dress; not an ornament is to be seen, except that simple little black cross, which gives the final touch to her interesting appearance, making her look like that most touching of all beings, a persecuted Roman Catholic young lady.

"What an interesting young creature!" says every one to every one. "Poor thing! how melancholy she looks! What can be her name?" "Eliza de Lacy," replies the lady of the house, highly delighted. "Eliza de Lacy. What a pretty name!" says each young lady who hears the disclosure, and straightway retires into a corner with some other young lady, to talk over the interesting pale unknown.

At an early hour the interesting young lady's papa comes from his rubber, puts a shawl of some unusual pattern round her very carefully, and marches her away. Every one feels relieved at her departure, and yet the interesting young lady has gained her end. She has produced a sensation. No sooner is she outside the door than she becomes perfectly natural and merry again—satirizes the two fat old ladies most unmercifully—retails all their scandal in the most piquant manner—quizzes the mistress of the house till her father splits his sides—and, finally, goes to bed with the delightful conviction that all the neighbourhood will be talking of her, more or less, for the next week to come.

𝕿HE 𝕻ETTING 𝖄OUNG 𝕷ADY

———◆———

𝖂ERE we to define the petting young lady, we should say that she is one who loves every living thing which is small. The fact of being small is quite sufficient to guarantee her affections without any additional requisite whatever. So strong is this love of hers for smallness in any shape, that her favourite term for expressing intense admiration is the word "little." Thus if she see a horse which pleases her she instantly cries out, "What a dear little horse!" although the horse be as big as a hay-stack; if a dog, "What a nice little dog!" if a house, "What a sweet little house!" Her whole language is a compound of diminutives. Instead of saying "mouse," she says "mousey;" instead of "aunt," "aunty;" instead of "shoe," "shoey." The petting young lady began her small existence with loving a little doll. When she was three years old she fell in love with a little lamb, an affection which lasted till the little lamb became a large sheep, on which act of insubordination she discarded him into the hands of the butcher. Her next attachment was a little dog, till the little dog became a big dog; on which she took a little canary and a little kitten. Of late she has been petting a little pony, till it is ready to burst: and finds no delight so great as in nursing a most particularly small baby belonging to the married housemaid, which she calls a sweet dear little thing, and half suffocates with hugging, at least a dozen times a day. If you call at the house you will be sure to find her in tribulation about some favourite. Either her chicken has broken its leg;

45

or her spaniel has shattered his constitution by tumbling off her lap upon the rug; or her pet pig has been slaughtered for salting; or her canary has been killed by the cat. It is quite surprising what a host of troubles she has; you would fancy her the mother of a dozen children at least.

And yet with all this excessive love for animals, a hundred to one but she is unkind towards her younger sisters, if she have any. Her selfishness knows no bounds. She is always appropriating. When you call, take care how you lead the conversation to zoology. She will be sure to coax you for a little Chinese pig, or a little Andalusian cat, or a little Mexican dog, the uglier the better. A much cheaper way of gaining her regard is to kiss severally each and all of her pets in regular rotation. This will be sure to please her, and when you go away, she may perhaps eulogistically say of you, if you are particularly lucky, "What a nice little man!"

THE NATURAL HISTORIAN YOUNG LADY

———•———

THE difference between the petting young lady and the natural historian young lady is, that while the petting young lady loves living small things, the natural historian young lady loves dead small things. But as insects (which are her particular forte) will not die on purpose for the natural historian young lady, and as they are of no use to her unless they are dead, it follows as a natural consequence that they must be killed. Now, the natural historian young lady is always a most surprisingly humane person; accordingly, to her infinite honour, she always contrives to kill the insects in the manner most agreeable to their feelings. Sometimes she drives a heated needle bolt through the head of a beetle, taking a humane caution to sever the spine; because, as she says, that is the seat of sensation. Sometimes she deluges a spoonful of oil over some other equally fortunate animal, which, she assures you, kills him directly; although, to be sure, his legs go on moving for five hours and upwards afterwards, owing, as she philosophically observes, merely to the muscular motion.

But when the natural historian young lady has a desire to be most particularly humane, she goes into the butler's pantry, and brings out a tumbler in the most mysterious-looking manner. This tumbler she deposits upside down on a piece of white paper, upon the table in the drawing-room. Then she goes to cook for half a dozen matches, which she lays by the side of the tumbler; and lights a small taper, which she deposits on the other side. Not being one of the initiated, you wonder what magical rite she can be about to perform. Once more she goes out, probably into her bed-room, and returns with three small live butterflies, the produce of her morning's natural historic excursion. These she tenderly places, one by one, under the tumbler, in the position most suitable to their personal comfort, and straightway lighting the matches, fills the tumbler with sulphur smoke. The three butterflies fly round and round the inside of the tumbler, vainly struggling in their agony to escape. The natural historian young lady looks on, well pleased to observe them become sensibly weaker and weaker. In this state she leaves them for an hour, while she goes to read the chapters in the Bible, and returning at the expiration of that time finds them still alive. What can the natural historian young lady do? She does what humanity prescribes. Instantly another bundle of matches is lighted and applied to the same tumbler; by which process, repeated two or three times more, the butterflies at last are dead, in less than eight hours after beginning to die. Upon this happy consummation, the young lady takes them out, drives a pin with the greatest unconcern through the middle of each, and fixes them like impaled criminals on a row of corks in the bottom drawer but one of her "museum."

Such is the principal business of the natural historian young lady's innocent existence; besides which, however, she cultivates botany and mineralogy in a small way. She has a *hortus siccus* of her own, containing two dandelions, a primrose, and three daisies, all in a dried state, and every one of them without exception her own collecting. She has one side of a drawer entirely devoted to a piece of copper ore, a piece of iron ore, a piece of glass, and a lump of coal in its natural state. In conversation, it is quite wonderful what hard words she will use; so long! and sounding like Greek at the least, if not Hebrew! And yet the natural historian young lady treats them just as familiarly as though they were common words of English extraction. It is quite delightful to hear her. But, after all, the most delightful thing in young ladies of this class is their skill in theorising. Such an accumulation of knowledge, to be sure, they bring to bear on their theories! and such theories! You would fancy them philosophers in petticoats. Their favourite theory of all is the insensibility to pain on the part of the brute creation, especially insects. A very comfortable theory certainly, so far as regards their own conscience, but possibly not quite so comfortable for the harmless insects which they destroy. And yet the natural historian young lady is not cruel. Far from it.

We have seen her cry, absolutely shed tears, when her own finger has been cut. And so far from possessing an instinctive love for the smoke of sulphur, she cannot even bear the parlour when it is full of common smoke. All this proves her to be a humane person, a very humane person; and yet we shall always most cautiously avoid tying ourselves for life to her; not because we think her cruel—far from it; but simply because we are afraid that, in case of our dying before her, she would cause us to be stuffed, and sent in a glass case to the British Museum as a natural historic curiosity.

THE INDIRECT YOUNG LADY

———•———

THERE is a sort of young lady altogether indigenous to this island, whom we call the indirect young lady, from her aversion to answer any question in a straightforward manner. You would almost suppose, from her answers to the commonest interrogatories, that she was a prisoner on trial at the Old Bailey.

The other day we had the singular fortune to fall in with a fair specimen of this class. She had lately, we knew, been at a ball. We expressed our hope that she had not caught cold in returning therefrom. "Why, as to that, Mr. P——," replied she, "really I don't know what to say; I may have caught a cold, and I may have not caught a cold. It's so difficult to know for certain." "Very true," said we at this most cautious piece of philosophic reply; "but how did you like the ball itself?" "Really," said the indirect young lady, "I am hardly

49

prepared to answer that question. Most of my friends seemed to like it very much." "Certainly," said we and, perceiving that on this point at least the young lady was determined not to commit herself, hastened to another topic of conversation, by seriously observing that it was a fine day. "Why," said she, "I hardly agree with you there. It isn't exactly fine—is it?" "Certainly not," said we; "but, by-the-bye, is it true that we are going to lose you, and that you are going to live in Hampshire?" "Really, Mr. P——," replied the indirect young lady, "I think Hampshire is a very pleasant county." "Very pleasant, indeed," said we, completely stopped on all sides from pursuing the conversation further: whereupon the indirect young lady commenced interrogatories on her side, and did not pause one second till she had gained from us definite answers to every piece of scandal that is going the round of the neighbourhood. We retired completely crest-fallen, and vowing most particularly that we would never again trust ourselves in company with the indirect young lady.

ᛏHE HYPERBOLICAL YOUNG LADY

———•———

ᛏHE hyperbolical young lady is one who exaggerates everything that she hears, sees, or does, till every separate act of her existence turns out to be an absolute miracle. There is always one hyperbolical young lady in every crowded neighbourhood, and she generally has an old father, or young brother, who at each of her several white lies constantly cry out, the one "Pish," and the other "Humbug;" whereupon the hyperbolical young lady turns invariably just slightly red in the face, and says angrily, "Well, I understood so, papa;" or "You never will believe anything, John."

We had long wondered how the hyperbolical young lady could always find subject-matter sufficient for her white lies, so as never to be at a loss the whole day. One morning we were detained by the rain, on a visit to her father. The hyperbolical young lady came in. "Only think," said she, "the rain has washed a hole in the roof just over our bed-room, at least a yard square." "How can you say such a thing, dear?" said papa; "you know that at this instant there are not enough drops come through to wet a towel." From danger by water the conversation turned to danger by fire. "I remember," said the hyperbolical young lady, "quite well, setting fire to a newspaper which I was holding before the fire to dry, when I was only two months old. What a fright it put me in!" "Very natural you should," said we; "it was a very providential escape." "Very odd, wasn't it?" said the hyperbolical young lady; "but what's odder, this morning the gardener found four dozen cock-sparrows all dead in a heap, under one gooseberry-bush. I thought I heard in the night a battle going on among the cock-sparrows, for the noise woke me." "There were only four sparrows, Lucy," chimed in brother John, "and that you know, as well as I. And what's more, I shot them before breakfast with my gun." "Then I suppose the gardener was mistaken, John," said the imperturbable Miss Lucy; "but what do you think, Mr. P——? when I was combing my hair, last night, more than ten million sparks came out of it, and flew all over the room like ever so many squibs. There was *such* a smell of fire!" "That's another banger," said John; "you

know you said, at breakfast, there was only one little spark."
"I will thank you, John, not to use that word," said our
hyperbolical friend, with dignity; "it's highly improper:
you're always teasing." Hereupon she commenced an
incipient blubber, and, having no relish for domestic broils,
we took our departure.

"What a pity," thought we, as we walked home, "that this
young lady, in other respects so amiable, has been suffered to
indulge a childish habit of exaggeration to such an extent,
that now her best friends can only excuse her of a vice by
denouncing her as a fool!"

The Whimsical Young Lady

————

The class of whimsical young ladies has been very much
on the increase of late in this kingdom, ever since the French
Revolution. In our inland county the two first specimens
appeared about ten years ago. Evidently they were not
indigenous; most persons supposed that they had migrated
from the West End. However that be, they took to the county
as if it had been natural to them, and presently led various
neighbouring young ladies to follow their peculiar habits
and instincts. Six years after their settlement, there were no
less than eleven young ladies of the county, to our certain
knowledge, become whimsical. The infection spread; and at
this present moment there is no village without its whimsical
young lady, who never knows her own mind for three minutes
together.

The Whimsical Young Lady

This singular animal may be known by the following characteristics:—She is always changing her purpose. Thus, having most particularly informed you that she requires you to walk out with her, you have no sooner prepared yourself with no small degree of extra attention, than you meet her at the bottom of the stairs in an in-door dress; and she informs you graciously that she is going to draw. Off you run for the portfolio, at her earnest request, and bring it back, out of breath, your new coat covered with a pleasant layer of dust from the cover. "I'm so sorry I gave you this trouble, Mr. Sparks," says the whimsical young lady, in the most enchanting manner possible. "I've just determined that drawing is a bore; and so you may take the portfolio back, if you please." You inwardly think that if drawing is a bore, the whimsical young lady is a greater bore; but as the whimsical young lady is generally good-looking (for it would by no means be the thing for a plain young lady to be whimsical), you console yourself as best you can, by considering that she would not have given you all this trouble if she didn't like you. Ill-fated supposition! for that you may not be ignorant, let me assure you that the same young lady exhibits her whimsicalities much more towards the maid-servant, "Jenny," than even towards your most noble self. "Jenny, I shall wear that Irish poplin this morning." "Yes, miss," says the obsequious Jenny, and brings the gown directed. The whimsical young lady gazes at it for an instant with intense delight. Of a sudden her countenance changes from no visible cause. "Stop, Jenny; I'm thinking that after all I won't wear the poplin. Just go and bring my merino, there's a good thing." Off goes Jenny, on a second excursion, and is no sooner come back than our whimsical lady cries out, "Don't bring that odious merino, Jenny; it will make me sick. The old black silk which aunt Mary gave me will do quite well enough." In this manner she sends Jenny through the whole wardrobe on a regular voyage of discovery. Then follows a long uncertainty on the manner in which her hair is dressed. The uncertainty ends in a conscientious conviction that the hair ought not to have been plaited as it is. The patient Jenny unplaits it, and "does" it in two, huge, staring, impudent bows, cocked over each eye. The whimsical young lady looks in the glass. The hair won't do yet. It must be plaited again into three tails, hanging down behind, and reminding you for all the world of a gentleman-farmer's cart-horse, in his Sunday best.

At breakfast it is all the same. When the question is first propounded to the whimsical young lady whether she will have bread or toast, she says "toast." The next moment she alters her mind, and says "bread." Then "toast" again; and so on through all the rest of that important meal.

But the queerest thing of all in the whimsical young lady is the rotation in which her various whims come. Sometimes she has a whim about one thing, which lasts three days; then about another, which lasts a week. There are some which keep by for a year,—others for an hour at most. A young lady of this class, an acquaintance of ours, was wholly unable to eat roast beef for seven weeks and three days; after which she took to it on a sudden, and liked nothing better. Soon afterwards she was attacked by another whim, which lasted four calendar months. 'Twas very strange, but somehow or other she couldn't help laughing whenever she heard the Old Hundredth. This was succeeded by a whim which lasted a year, and consisted in an unconquerable antipathy to cows.

All this time, whenever she saw a cow, large or little, black or white, with horns or without horns, she always fell into a fright. You would think it a case of animal magnetism. Yet no sooner was the year out, than she walked through a whole drove of bullocks as unconcerned as an elephant.

Such are the singular phenomena which exhibit themselves in the whimsical young lady, and from a deep consideration of which we have been led to classify whims in the following manner:—First, the whim ephemeral; secondly, the whim hebdomadal; thirdly, the lunar whim, or whim which is comprised in a revolution of the moon; fourthly, the solar whim, or whim which lasts a year. Not to speak of those singular whims which, like comets, have no orbit yet discovered, but come and depart without warning, the greatest philosophers on earth not being able to pronounce when they will return.

THE ABSTEMIOUS YOUNG LADY

———•———

THERE is a class of young ladies, not uncommon, whom we denominate "the abstemious young ladies." This sisterhood seem to live, by all accounts, on air, and nothing else. You never see them eat, and yet they are tolerably stout too. We have known them weigh from eleven to twelve stone, which is pretty well for an abstemious young lady. At a dinner party they leave everything on their plate, after just picking up a morsel not sufficient for a tom-tit. Observe how daintily they hold their knife and fork—just by the extreme end of the handle—so that, even if they were disposed to that vulgar habit of eating, they could not lift up more than one grain avoirdupois. The lady of the house is continually pressing them to eat, with the most anxious solicitude for their well-being. "Really, Miss Carolina, you must eat something. Take a piece of boiled turkey: do, pray. A little bit of roast beef. John, take Miss Carolina Webster's plate for a slice of beef." "Really, Mrs. Hopkins," answers the abstemious young lady, "I do assure you I have made a most excellent dinner. I never eat more. Ask mamma." Hereupon Mrs. Hopkins, with anxiety quite maternal, interrogates Mrs. Webster touching and concerning "poor" Carolina's appetite; to which Mrs. Webster replies with dignity—"I can assure you, Mrs. Hopkins, that what Carolina says is quite true. She is a very little eater—a very, very little eater indeed." This settles the matter.

In our juvenile days we used frequently to come in for these sort of colloquies, and yet invariably could not fail of observing that the abstemious young lady, despite of what her mother said about her little eating, was always, without exception, the fattest young lady in the room. This inconsistency used to puzzle our philosophical brains most completely. "How can this be?" thought we. "By what miraculous intervention, by what freak of Nature does it come to pass, that the fattest young lady is always the one who eats least?" We considered and re-considered the case, but could find no answer. At last, in sheer desperation, we determined upon putting the matter to a test, by watching closely the young lady herself. "Who knows," thought we, "but there is some sort of invaluable gas which the abstemious young lady inhales every morning; or perhaps she lives on

The Abstemious Young Lady

milk and arrowroot; or, most likely of all, she lives, like a snipe, by suction, and only feeds on juices." Our desperate resolution was fixed. We determined to thrust ourselves suddenly into the presence of the abstemious young lady, when she least expected it, and by a bold stroke to solve the problem. There only wanted an excuse for breaking in upon the abstemious young lady's private existence. We procured from our sister Letitia a piece of new music, which the abstemious young lady had expressed a wish to see, and thus armed, between the hours of one and two, started on our adventurous excursion, and thrust ourselves, unannounced, slap into the parlour.

Our doubts were resolved in an instant, but not in the way which we expected. We beheld no gas—no arrowroot—no suction. At a large table, surrounded by her younger sisters (each a fat pattern of herself in their various degrees of size), sat the abstemious young lady. In a large dish before her lay the mangled remains of a huge leg of mutton. She herself was devouring with all her might, doubtless as an example to the younger ones. She was rather chagrined, it was clear, at our approach. But we were too juvenile to notice things. So, at least, she seemed to consider on second thoughts; for telling the maid-servant to set a chair, she first helped us, and then continued eating without stopping once till her plate was cleared. How was our small mind surprised at beholding that mouth, which we had considered as sealed for ever, now employed in the full operation of gormandising! We sate in silent wonder. A large round plum-pudding came in: the abstemious young lady helped each of her sisters to a small piece, then us to a large piece, and then herself to a larger. We were thirsty: she gave us a tumbler-full from her own jug. We drank,—it was porter. The cloth was removed, and then the abstemious young lady found time to inform us that she always carved for the children, and made her own little luncheon at the same time. "I had thought it was your dinner," said we simply. "By no means," said the abstemious young lady.

The mystery was explained. We returned home another person, a foot higher at the least. Such was the success of our first philosophical inquiry into the phenomena of the young lady creation.

The Sincere Young Lady

———◆———

THERE is a class of young ladies rapidly hastening to extinction, who make a point of always, in every circumstance, speaking exactly what they think. They really seem to suppose that every one likes to be told the truth, and have evidently formed the unphilosophical idea that not to say everything you think is as criminal as to say what you do not think.

This theory is always gaining enemies for the sincere young lady. "How do I look this morning, dear?" says her aunt. "Why, aunt," replies the sincere young lady, "if you ask me, I must say that I think you look older than usual." "Very glad to see you," says Mr. Augustus Johnson. "I don't believe it," says the sincere young lady. "Pray, why did not you and your mother dine with us last Thursday?" asks Mrs. Rackett. "The truth is," answers the sincere young lady, "we had a more pleasant engagement."

But the most unpleasant thing in the sincere young lady is her volunteering truths without being asked at all. The other day we were singing a duet with the abstemious young lady. Up comes the sincere young lady, and says, in a compassionate tone, "You don't sing nearly so well as you used." "Miss Dobson likes chicken so we have got one on purpose," says the good-natured Mrs. Starks. "I dislike it particularly," says the sincere young lady.

With all this, however, we cannot help allowing that if we dislike the sincere young lady, we respect her no less. She has a high idea of truth: and, like few of her sex, may be trusted with a secret in a case of emergency. The pity is that she cannot distinguish, and thus often hurts the little vanities of people at the very time when she is most studious of their regard.

The Affirmative Young Lady

The affirmative young lady is just contrary to the sincere young lady, and is so fond of pleasing that, at the expense of truth, she is willing to agree with every one. That touching and expressive monosyllable "yes" is always on her lips. She not only answers every interrogatory with it, but even intersperses it among her own sentences at every fifth word. Her genius is shown chiefly in lengthening and shortening its pronunciation, in such a manner as to express the different modifications of affirmation. She can whine it out in such a lengthy, dubious manner, "y—e—s," as to make it signify almost "no." She can pronounce it deliberately "yes," as the result of patient investigation. Or she can repeat it hurriedly several times together, "yes, yes, yes," denoting impatience. In short, her ways of using the word "yes" are so various that she may be said to have been born with "yes" in her mouth, and to have lived upon "yes" ever since; thus giving a capital chance to all matrimonial pretenders; and, as it were, practising beforehand for that most important "yes" to which we are assured all young ladies look forward so aspiringly. "You have a nice garden," said we one day to the affirmative young lady. "Y-e-s," replied she, "it is a very nice garden; yes, a particularly nice garden; yes, but your garden is better; yes, a great deal better; yes."

The affirmative young lady is generally esteemed most especially good-natured, yet we hold that her disposition to agree with every one is in fact rather the result of a disinclination to be bored. There is nothing so absurd but she will agree to it, if you propound it to her. Right or wrong, it's all one to her, so that she hear no more of it. Some persons think that she is treacherous, and humours every one merely that she may laugh at them the more behind their backs. We don't think so. Such a design is too deep to be attributed to her. Besides, she really likes to see people at ease with themselves, and thinks it her duty to make every one as happy as possible, which is the reason why she was never known to say an unkind thing, or what could in any manner hurt the feelings of another.

Alas! that she will not use one small grain of judgement, and try to be a little respected, when she is so sure of being beloved.

The Clever Young Lady

—◆—

ONE of our favourite characters among young ladies is the clever young lady, the only one of young ladies who unites a complete milliner's education with a knowledge of things in general. She will read you out Silvio Pellico into good English, at the same time that she is making a cap on new principles for her grandmother. She always makes all her own dresses in the most elegant style imaginable; has been known to turn her straw bonnet twice, and make it look better for the change each time; and yet all this does not prevent her from keeping an album full of the wittiest and most pathetic things in the world, half of which she wrote herself off-hand, with the most ludicrous illustrations done with her own pen, as well as Phiz himself.

Then she always knows the population of every town, and the name of every village within a hundred miles round, and has got all the neighbouring M.P.'s pat in her recollection. You may ask her any question you please, and she will answer you better than any one else in the room, notwithstanding the young gentleman from Cambridge is present. Her chronology is perfect, from Noah to last Monday: you would think she had a little almanack packed snug in some corner of her brain; and yet you wouldn't believe it! but she invented her own chronological system herself. Observe her writing: what a beautifully neat hand! and so talented! as the literary young lady says. Then she is always inventing some pretty toy for the children. And at the last fancy fair, more than half the things and all the best of them, were made by her. There is no odd or end, from silk to canvas, which she cannot convert into a perfect treasure.

By-the-bye, speaking of that fancy fair, it was she who set it all going. Who would have thought it possible to get up a real fancy fair in this village? And yet the clever young lady managed it, and very well too, ma'am, let me tell you. Who was it but she that caused her father's antiquated barn to be decked out so prettily for the occasion? And then, when the company came, wasn't she everywhere at the same time, raising the prices, and saying witty things on each article? especially that remarkably witty thing which she said to a gentleman, who was looking very earnestly in the direction of her stall. For, thinking that he was looking at a blue pin-cushion, she said to him, "That's half-a-crown;" to which, when the gentleman answered, "I was not looking at the pin-cushion, but at you"—"That," said the clever young lady, "is five shillings." Thus by her industry alone she raised the sum of twelve pounds ten and sevenpence, all for the poor: and every one knows to this day, that all the articles together were not worth fifteen shillings.

But perhaps you might think the clever young lady superficial. No such thing. Let me tell you, sir, that although she doesn't show it, sir, she knows all Genesis in Hebrew, and has read more German divines than the literary young lady herself, sir. But, sir, the fact is, she has such good taste that she knows better than to intrude upon any one her knowledge either of Hebrew, or German or music or conchology, or heraldry, or botany, or French, each of which she knows much better than a hundred gentlemen pretenders. Then, too, what delightful crust she can make! It is quite an era in one's life to eat one of those little caraway biscuits—her own recipe, by-the-bye. Such a useful person, too, she is in the parish!—our new curate positively couldn't get on without her. Some say indeed that he is so aware of this, he is determined to have her for his own property altogether—but this is between you and me. Who is it but she that gives him lists of the old men who want flannel waistcoats, and the young girls who want to get into the Sunday school? We declare upon our honour that we never knew such a useful, such an invaluable young lady; and when we say this for her, we say a great deal for her, let me tell you, miss,—for young ladies are not generally useful creatures, but much oftener in the way, miss; and, besides, she is very amiable and unaffected, too, and always doing good; so that at this present moment there is no young lady to whom we wish better, or whom we admire more, than the clever young lady.

THE MYSTERIOUS YOUNG LADY

———◆———

THE mysterious young lady has so strong a natural partiality for secrets, that she was never known to tell one, unless it were to gain another. Not that she has anything in the world which is of vital importance to keep secret, but she is of opinion that her own dignity is materially increased by her being supposed to know anything which to the generality is unknown.

On this principle, whatever is told her, whether in confidence or not, she instantly converts into a secret, just as a miser turns everything into gold. She laughs: some one asks the reason. "A secret," says she. She looks melancholy: you ask what's the matter. "I mayn't tell," says she. Everything with her is a mystery. 'Tis quite surprising out of what trivial matters she will play the Machiavel. Her very movements are mysterious. Sometimes she will walk four times in a morning down the village and back again, apparently in great haste. All the neighbouring windows are in a state of excitement. "What *can* Miss Wells be after? Something important must be going on—either the flannel waistcoats are to be distributed, or the new penny reading books." By no means. The mysterious young lady merely walked backwards and forwards in this manner to create a sensation, and—increase her dignity. After tea, when the ladies are working together in front of the fire, on a sudden down flops the mysterious young lady on the carpet. "What have you lost?" cry each and all. "Something," says the mysterious young lady; "I can find it myself." Presently she emerges from under the table, with a red face and a self-satisfied expression. She has found what she dropped, but what that was, no one is ever informed, and no one knows to this day.

The mysterious young lady never tells beforehand what she is going to do. You do not know that she is going out walking till you see her with her bonnet on; and as to which way she is going, you may puzzle your brains as much as you please, but we will defy you to discover by hook or by crook. When she is going to a place, she never starts the direct way.

Such is the mysterious young lady every day of her life. But when there is really a secret of importance committed to her, which happens about once in two years,—just mark her then. Such a solemn look!—such a screwed-up mouth to prevent the secret escaping! She looks more full of secrets than the sphinx of Egypt itself.

Her great forte, however, lies in her manner of opening a letter at breakfast. Mark how seriously she breaks the seal,—how composedly she unfolds the epistle,—and, without saying a single word, commences reading with the most intense interest. When she has finished, every one asks the news. "What news, love?" says mamma. "Anything about John?" says papa. "What does Amelia say?" says Tom. The mysterious young lady solemnly shakes her head, and to each question answers with dignity, "Nothing—no news at all—nothing, nothing." Here little Jenny asks simply whom the letter is from. The mysterious young lady deigns no answer. The general impatience increases—the dignity of the mysterious young lady is at its height. By degrees she lets out the news bit by bit. First, whom the letter is from; then the date; then the place; then the first piece of news; then the second, and so on, enjoying her dignity to the last. When the news is all told, and others want to read the letter, she always insinuates that there is a particular secret reserved for herself, which she wishes no one else to know; and by this manœuvre regains at once all her former dignity. Mamma smiles. Papa cries "Pish! nonsense!" Sisters begin to howl. The mysterious young lady is inflexible—and finally destroys all further hope of gaining the secret, by depositing the letter in her desk, within that most secret and mysterious drawer, which the prying eyes of no mortal have yet seen into, except little Sam for one second, by creeping under the table; in return for which impertinence he received a certain hard box on the ear, which till this time he has not forgot, although it is a full year ago.

THE EXTREMELY NATURAL YOUNG LADY

———•———

FAR be it from us to deny that the fair sex are exhibited to most advantage, when they throw off artificials and appear in their natural character. But there is a class who like so much to have it said of them "How very natural!" that they become affected on purpose.

The extremely natural young lady is always doing some out-of-the-way thing, that she may appear simple and girlish. She is most particularly fond of romping; and, when you are out walking with her, is sure to run after a small donkey, or jump a ditch, or have her fortune told, or thrust herself bolt through a hedge; all which little exhibitions she esteems to be beautiful and touching pieces of rustic elegance. Then suppose she is able to sing, and comes to a green lane, forthwith she begins chirruping like a young sparrow; and if a cart pass by at that particular time, ten to one she jumps in and tells the boy to make the horses gallop. She enjoys nothing so much as getting her gown torn, and is particularly fond of arranging her hair out of doors. We have known her stop on a common, give us her bonnet and cap to hold, and proceed to her toilet in the most simple, unaffected manner possible; all so delightfully natural; it was quite pleasant to see her setting her curls in their places, and wagging about her head right and left. When the natural young lady is in doors, she is always running out of doors, especially if it rains—*that* is

The Extremely Natural Young Lady

perfection. She is delighted above all things with making snowballs. If there be a cow within a mile, she is sure to go some morning before breakfast and drink the warm milk, a feat of which she never ceases to talk for three months after. She will box a gentleman's ears and think nothing of it. She was never known to walk, but always hops and skips. Her utmost ambition is to be called a wild thing. This makes her talk frequently in a very odd manner, especially to gentlemen. She will tell Mr. Cripps that he looks particularly well, whereupon Mr. Cripps smiles, and is straightway informed that he looks particularly well for Mr. Cripps.

If we are ever to fall in love, in this late season of our existence, preserve us from falling in love with the extremely natural young lady.

THE LAZY YOUNG LADY

———•———

As in the brute creation nature has created the sloth, the use of which animal our zoologists have never been able to discover,—so in the young lady creation we find an analogous class, whom from their habits we denominate the lazy young lady (*Domina pigra*).

The lazy young lady was never known to get through the pronunciation of an ordinary monosyllable in less than thirty seconds. Assuredly she must have a wonderful taste for the beauties of language, for from her drawl it is plain that she is determined on enjoying as long as she can every word that she utters, just as a prudent economical child sucks his barley-sugar instead of biting it to pieces at once. Then observe the lazy young lady's attitude. Such a perfect lounge on the very easiest and lowest chair which she can pick out. We verily believe she knows every chair in the room by its comparative softness, or possibly (as we have sometimes thought) she may have been born with an intuitive power of knowing the easiest chair at first sight. If it is winter, too, her cheeks are always most particularly red, from her custom of dragging the said chair as near to the fire as possible, and sitting there for hours, with her feet on the fender, buried in huge worsted shoes, which remind you of the north pole and Captain Ross.

The lazy young lady is sometimes thin and sometimes fat, but generally the latter. On any sudden concussion her cheeks will shiver like a jelly. If you will believe her, she always has a headache; but for our own part, we strongly suspect that this headache is very often a pure invention to gratify her lazy propensities. It is quite delightful to hear her colloquies with "mamma." "My dear, run and tell Betty that I want her directly." "Hadn't I better ring the bell, mamma?" says the lazy young lady. "No, my dear, you know that your uncle Tom is ill, and the bell might wake him—go yourself." "Yes, mamma," drawls the lazy young lady and drags herself along to the door at the rate of the minute-hand of her own watch. At the door, however, her resolution to go all the way to Betty (who perhaps may be upstairs making the beds) fails her completely. To mount those pyramidical stairs is too awful a prospect. Accordingly, she stops at the bottom, and bawls out as loudly as she can, "Betty, Betty, mamma wants you—make haste!" This done, she crawls back, like an old woman of a hundred, to her easy chair, and flings herself down, in a most terrible state of fatigue from her late exertions.

The Lazy Young Lady

Presently the clock strikes eleven. "Now, my dear," says mamma, "go and practise." "The clock on the stairs hasn't struck yet," says the lazy young lady. At last the clock on the stairs strikes. The lazy young lady makes two efforts to rise from her chair without success. One would think that some invisible power held her back. "Oh, mamma," she cries out at length, "mayn't I put off practising till twelve? It will do just as well." "No, my dear," says mamma, who knows perfectly well, from experience, how cunning the lazy young lady can be when she wants to put off business; "no, my dear, go at once." The lazy young lady waddles off at this authoritative admonition, casting many a wistful glance backwards at the easy chair. You hear her sigh as she opens the door, which she closes with a bang, to save trouble. If you listen sharply, you will now hear heavy feet dragging slowly upstairs. Presently a low monotonous sound comes through the ceiling from the study, as of somebody practising on the pianoforte. At first it is tolerably quick. Allegro perhaps, but never presto. From allegro, it subsides in a few minutes to allegretto, and so to andante. Mamma listens with painful attention. What can be the matter? Now only two or three notes are heard at wide intervals. Now the music has stopped altogether. Up jumps mamma, and is met at the door by the lazy young lady returning from her practising. "What's this, Amelia?" says mamma; "you haven't been practising ten minutes." "I thought it was an hour," says the lazy young lady. "I am *so* tired, mamma, I really can't practise any more now." By this time she has reached the fire. The easy chair is too tempting. Down she flops, and remains there in the same position, till she is forced to go and dress for dinner. By the time dinner is half over she comes back. Everything is cold. Papa scolds, mamma frowns, brothers frown, and call her "lag last." "Why can't you be quicker?" says mamma. "Really, mamma," says the lazy young lady, "I came as quickly as I could. I ran all the way downstairs."

ᵀHE ᵞOUNG ᴸADY ᶠROM ˢCHOOL

⸻•⸻

ᵀHE young ladies from school are a class of human beings whom, we flatter ourselves, we know the instant they are presented to our cognisance. We can even tell at a glance how long they have been at school; how long they have to stay; whether their school is in London or the country; whether it is a finishing school, or a beginning school, or a middling school; whether the mistress is an old maid or a widow; and whether there are many young ladies at the said school, or only a few young ladies. All this we know from our first glance at a young lady from school.

If a young lady be really and truly at school, and not a mere private pupil (which is a sort of neutral animal), you may be sure that she has not yet come out, and that she has not yet come out you may easily know, by observing whether she dined with the company, or only came in to tea. Besides, young ladies who have not come out seem always out of their place, and are so intolerably fidgety on their chairs, that you would think the cushions must be red-hot to make them shift about so.

But the young lady from school is still more easily known, from her conversation with some other young lady who never was at school, or has just left school. Listen for a moment, and you will find that their whole discourse just now turns on Miss Simkins, the new governess, whom, you may easily perceive, the young lady from school most heartily detests. Presently the conversation shifts to an account of the new-comers of "last half," Miss Shuffles, Miss Hopkins, Miss Louisa Tubbs, and Miss Jenny Hogg. Such a nice dear little thing is that little Jenny! Then follows a long detail of the French books which they read now in the first class, which is succeeded in due time by a serious quizzing of all the company present. We have studied the subject carefully, and aver that all your young ladies from school are quizzes without exception. And yet, you wouldn't think it, but each is *so* bashful, when a gentleman comes up and speaks to her, always calling him Sir, and after each reply, looking down slap upon her toes. To be fair, however, we confess that this is only just at first. In the course of five minutes, when you are more acquainted, she runs on at a surprising rate of tongue; and if you are disposed to draw her out, will tell you *such* stories of wicked deeds done at school! How one of the young ladies gathered an apple, out walking, by getting on the top of a stile; how another stole a little kitten, and carried it home in her muff, and kept it three whole days on gingerbread, in her bedroom, inside a band-box; how three of the elder ones, in concert, bribed old Sally with two and ninepence, and walked all the way to the fair after tea, to buy some sugar-candy, and *such* nice sugar-candy! With these, and such-like little histories, she will divert you exceedingly.

Then it is quite ludicrous to see her walk; always endeavouring to walk as the posture-mistress, and not as nature taught her, till finally nature gets the better of the posture-mistress, and the young lady from school walks for a brief moment like other two-legged beings. Observe, too, those two expressions so common with her,—"We always do so at Miss La Trobe's;" "We never do so at Miss La Trobe's;" mark how she introduces the touching words "last half" in every other sentence; watch her affectionate fondness for tarts and "nice things;" and if, after all this, you cannot pronounce any given young lady in the universe to be, or not to be, a young lady from school, we give you up as a blockhead, fit to return to school yourself, and stay there too, vacations and all.

CONCLUSION

HERE we pause, after having described, to the best of our zoological powers, two dozen classes of young ladies. Far be it from us even to hint that we have exhausted the precious store, which, as we have before observed, we conceive to be co-extensive with the most unlimited works of nature, both in point of number and variety. All that we pretend to say is, that we have selected the most striking and important classes at this present time existing in Great Britain. We candidly confess that we have even passed over many classes of great weight in society, not through ignorance, but for fear of wearying the reader's attention with too long a catalogue even of young ladies. Thus we have not considered in the least either the over-particular young lady, or the common-place young lady, or the passionate young lady, or the shop-going young lady, or the obstinate young lady, or the flirting young lady, or the young lady of feeling, or the married young lady, or the young lady who is an old maid, or the old maid who is a young lady; all of which classes, it must be confessed, exercise a great influence on the fate of Great Britain in general, and their own villages in particular.

Enough has been done, however, to show the extent and philosophy of the subject in a fair proportion; and if the young ladies themselves shall confess that, on the whole, we have been true to nature in our researches, there is no higher praise which we desire. Doubtless some gentlemen will accuse us of exhibiting the young lady creation in by no means the most amiable of all possible colours. To this we plead guilty, but must add in our justification, that the general excellence of the youthful fair constrained us, if we would describe them, to have recourse to particular foibles. Moreover, we do hope and trust that this treatise is to work some good even among the young ladies themselves, who, as a body, we love and admire too much to conceal from them what it is that makes them sometimes to be ridiculous with all their good qualities.

Let us hope that the young ladies for once will forgive us for trying to serve them a good turn, especially as we engage ever after from this time to praise them up to the skies, and down again too, if they so desire.

SKETCHES OF YOUNG GENTLEMEN

WITH ILLUSTRATIONS BY PHIZ

Sketches

OF

Young Gentlemen.

Dedicated to the Young Ladies.

WITH SIX ILLUSTRATIONS

BY

"PHIZ."

TO THE YOUNG LADIES

OF THE

𝔘𝔫𝔦𝔱𝔢𝔡 𝔎𝔦𝔫𝔤𝔡𝔬𝔪 𝔬𝔣 𝔊𝔯𝔢𝔞𝔱 𝔅𝔯𝔦𝔱𝔞𝔦𝔫 𝔞𝔫𝔡 𝔍𝔯𝔢𝔩𝔞𝔫𝔡;

ALSO

THE YOUNG LADIES

OF

THE PRINCIPALITY OF WALES,

AND LIKEWISE

THE YOUNG LADIES

RESIDENT IN THE ISLES OF

𝔊𝔲𝔢𝔯𝔫𝔰𝔢𝔶, 𝔍𝔢𝔯𝔰𝔢𝔶, 𝔄𝔩𝔡𝔢𝔯𝔫𝔢𝔶, 𝔞𝔫𝔡 𝔖𝔞𝔯𝔨,

THE HUMBLE DEDICATION OF THEIR DEVOTED ADMIRER,

SHEWETH,—

𝕿HAT your Dedicator has perused, with feelings of virtuous indignation, a work purporting to be "Sketches of Young Ladies;" written by Quiz, illustrated by Phiz, and published in one volume, square twelvemo.

THAT after an attentive and vigilant perusal of the said work, your Dedicator is humbly of opinion that so many libels, upon your Honourable sex were never contained in any previously published work, in twelvemo or any other mo.

THAT in the title page and preface to the said work, your Honourable sex are described and classified as animals; and although your Dedicator is not at present prepared to deny that you *are* animals, still he humbly submits that it is not polite to call you so.

THAT in the aforesaid preface, your honourable sex are also described as Troglodites, which, being a hard word, may, for aught your Honourable sex or your Dedicator can say to the contrary, be an injurious and disrespectful appellation.

THAT the author of the said work applied himself to his task in malice prepense and with wickedness aforethought; a fact which, your Dedicator contends, is sufficiently demonstrated, by his assuming the name of Quiz, which, your Dedicator submits, denotes a foregone conclusion, and implies an intention of quizzing.

THAT in the execution of his evil design, the said Quiz, or author of the said work, must have betrayed some trust or confidence reposed in him by some members of your Honourable sex, otherwise he never could have acquired so much information relative to the manners and customs of your Honourable sex in general.

THAT actuated by these considerations, and further moved by various slanders and insinuations respecting your Honourable sex contained in the said work, square twelvemo, entitled "Sketches of Young Ladies," your Dedicator ventures to produce another work, square twelvemo, entitled "Sketches of Young Gentlemen," of which he now solicits your acceptance and approval.

THAT as the Young Ladies are the best companions of the Young Gentlemen, so the Young Gentlemen should be the best companions of the Young Ladies; and extending the comparison from animals (to quote the disrespectful language of the said Quiz) to inanimate objects, your Dedicator humbly suggests, that such of your Honourable sex as purchased the bane should possess themselves of the antidote, and that those of your Honourable sex who were not rash enough to take the first, should lose no time in swallowing the last,—prevention being in all cases better than cure, as we are informed upon the authority, not only of general acknowledgement, but also of traditionary wisdom.

THAT with reference to the said bane and antidote, your Dedicator has no further remarks to make, than are comprised in the printed directions issued with Doctor Morison's pills; namely, that whenever your Honourable sex take twenty-five of Number 1, you will be pleased to take fifty of Number 2, without delay.

And your Dedicator shall ever pray, &c.

CONTENTS

—◆—

ℒist of ℐllustrations

THE BASHFUL YOUNG GENTLEMAN

———•———

WE found ourself seated at a small dinner party, the other day, opposite a stranger of such singular appearance and manner, that he irresistibly attracted our attention.

This was a fresh-coloured young gentleman, with as good a promise of light whisker as one might wish to see, and possessed of a very velvet-like soft-looking countenance. We do not use the latter term invidiously, but merely to denote a pair of smooth, plump, highly-coloured cheeks of capacious dimensions, and a mouth rather remarkable for the fresh hue of the lips than for any marked or striking expression it presented. His whole face was suffused with a crimson blush, and bore that downcast, timid, retiring look, which betokens a man ill at ease with himself.

There was nothing in these symptoms to attract more than a passing remark, but our attention had been originally drawn to the bashful young gentleman, on his first appearance in the drawing-room above-stairs, into which he was no sooner introduced, than making his way towards us who were standing in a window, and wholly neglecting several persons who warmly accosted him, he seized our hand with visible emotion, and pressed it with a convulsive grasp for a good couple of minutes, after which he dived in a nervous manner across the room, oversetting in his way a fine little girl of six years and a quarter old—and shrouding himself behind some hangings, was seen no more, until the eagle eye of the hostess detecting him in his concealment, on the announcement of dinner, he was requested to pair off with a lively single lady, of two or three and thirty.

This most flattering salutation from a perfect stranger would have gratified us not a little, as a token of his having held us in high respect, and for that reason been desirous of our acquaintance, if we had not suspected from the first that the young gentleman, in making a desperate effort to get through the ceremony of introduction, had, in the bewilderment of his ideas, shaken hands with us at random. This impression was fully confirmed by the subsequent behaviour of the bashful young gentleman in question, which we noted particularly, with the view of ascertaining whether we were right in our conjecture.

The young gentleman seated himself at table with evident misgivings, and turning sharp round to pay attention to some observation of his loquacious neighbour, overset his bread. There was nothing very bad in this, and if he had had the presence of mind to let it go, and say nothing about it, nobody but the man who had laid the cloth would have been a bit the wiser; but the young gentleman in various semi-successful attempts to prevent its fall, played with it a little, as gentlemen in the streets may be seen to do with their hats on a windy day, and then giving the roll a smart rap in his anxiety to catch it, knocked it with great adroitness into a tureen of white soup at some distance, to the unspeakable terror and disturbance of a very amiable bald gentleman, who was dispensing the contents. We thought the bashful young gentleman would have gone off in an apoplectic fit, consequent upon the violent rush of blood to his face at the occurrence of this catastrophe.

From this moment we perceived, in the phraseology of the fancy, that it was "all up" with the bashful young gentleman, and so indeed it was. Several benevolent persons endeavoured to relieve his embarrassment by taking wine with him, but finding that it only augmented his sufferings, and that after mingling sherry, champagne, hock, and moselle together, he applied the greater part of the mixture externally, instead of internally, they gradually dropped off, and left him to the exclusive care of the talkative lady, who not noting the wildness of his eye, firmly believed she had secured a listener. He broke a glass or two in the course of the meal, and disappeared shortly afterwards; it is inferred that he went away in some confusion, inasmuch as he left the house in another gentleman's coat, and the footman's hat.

This little incident led us to reflect upon the most prominent characteristics of bashful young gentlemen in the abstract; and as this portable volume will be the great text-book of young ladies in all future generations, we record them here for their guidance and behoof.

If the bashful young gentleman, in turning a street corner, chance to stumble suddenly upon two or three young ladies of his acquaintance, nothing can exceed his confusion and agitation. His first impulse is to make a great variety of bows, and dart past them, which he does until, observing that they wish to stop, but are uncertain whether to do so or not, he makes several feints of returning, which causes them to do the same; and at length, after a great quantity of unnecessary dodging and falling up against the other passengers, he returns and shakes hands most affectionately with all of them, in doing which he knocks out of their grasp sundry little parcels, which he hastily picks up, and returns very muddy and disordered. The chances are that the bashful young gentleman then observes it is very fine weather, and being reminded that it has only just left off raining for the first time these three days, he blushes very much, and smiles as if he had said a very good thing. The young lady who was most anxious to speak here inquires, with an air of great commiseration, how his dear sister Harriet is today; to which the young gentleman, without the slightest consideration, replies with many thanks, that she is remarkably well. "Well, Mr. Hopkins!" cries the young lady, "why, we heard she was bled yesterday evening, and have been perfectly miserable about her." "Oh, ah," says the young gentleman, "so she was. Oh, she's very ill, very ill indeed." The young gentleman then shakes his head, and looks very desponding (he has been smiling perpetually up to this time), and after a short pause, gives his glove a great wrench at the wrist, and says, with a strong emphasis on the adjective, "*Good* morning, *good* morning." And making a great number of bows in acknowledgment of several little messages to his sister, walks backward a few paces, and comes with great violence against a lamp-post, knocking his hat off in the contact, which in his mental confusion and bodily pain he is going to walk away without, until a great roar from a carter attracts his attention, when he picks it up, and tries to smile cheerfully to the young ladies, who are looking back, and who, he has the satisfaction of seeing, are all laughing heartily.

At a quadrille party, the bashful young gentleman always remains as near the entrance of the room as possible, from which position he smiles at the people he knows as they come in, and sometimes steps forward to shake hands with more intimate friends: a process which on each repetition seems to turn him a deeper scarlet than before. He declines dancing the first set or two, observing, in a faint voice, that he would rather wait a little; but at length is absolutely compelled to allow himself to be introduced to a partner, when he is led, in a great heat and blushing furiously, across the room to a spot where half-a-dozen unknown ladies are congregated together.

"Miss Lambert, let me introduce Mr. Hopkins for the next quadrille." Miss Lambert inclines her head graciously. Mr. Hopkins bows, and his fair conductress disappears, leaving Mr. Hopkins, as he too well knows, to make himself agreeable. The young lady more than half expects that the bashful young gentleman will say something, and the bashful young gentleman feeling this, seriously thinks whether he has got anything to say, which, upon mature reflection, he is rather disposed to conclude he has not, since nothing occurs to him. Meanwhile, the young lady, after several inspections of her bouquet, all made in the expectation that the bashful young gentleman is going to talk, whispers her mama, who is sitting next her, which whisper the bashful young gentleman immediately suspects (and possibly with very good reason) must be about *him*. In this comfortable condition he remains until it is time to "stand up," when murmuring a "Will you allow me?" he gives the young lady his arm, and after inquiring where she will stand, and receiving a reply that she has no choice, conducts her to the remotest corner of the quadrille, and making one attempt at conversation, which turns out a desperate failure, preserves a profound silence until it is all over, when he walks her twice round the room, deposits her in her old seat, and retires in confusion.

A married bashful gentleman—for these bashful gentlemen *do* get married sometimes; how it is ever brought about, is a mystery to us—a married bashful gentleman either causes his wife to appear bold by contrast, or merges her proper importance in his own insignificance. Bashful young gentlemen should be cured, or avoided. They are never hopeless, and never will be, while female beauty and attractions retain their influence, as any young lady will find, who may think it worth while on this confident assurance to take a patient in hand.

THE OUT-AND-OUT YOUNG GENTLEMAN

———•———

OUT-AND-OUT young gentlemen may be divided into two classes—those who have something to do, and those who have nothing. I shall commence with the former, because that species come more frequently under the notice of young ladies, whom it is our province to warn and to instruct.

The out-and-out young gentleman is usually no great dresser, his instructions to his tailor being all comprehended in the one general direction to "make that what's-a-name a regular bang-up sort of thing." For some years past, the favourite costume of the out-and-out young gentleman has been a rough pilot coat, with two gilt hooks and eyes to the velvet collar; buttons somewhat larger than crown-pieces; a black or fancy neckerchief, loosely tied; a wide-brimmed hat, with a low crown; tightish inexpressibles, and iron-shod boots. Out of doors he sometimes carries a large ash stick, but only on special occasions, for he prefers keeping his hands in his coat pockets. He smokes at all hours, of course, and swears considerably.

The Out-and-out Young Gentleman

The out-and-out young gentleman is employed in a city counting-house or solicitor's office, in which he does as little as he possibly can: his chief places of resort are, the streets, the taverns, and the theatres. In the streets at evening time, out-and-out young gentlemen have a pleasant custom of walking six or eight abreast, thus driving females and other inoffensive persons into the road, which never fails to afford them the highest satisfaction, especially if there be any immediate danger of their being run over, which enhances the fun of the thing materially. In all places of public resort, the out-and-outers are careful to select each a seat to himself, upon which he lies at full length, and (if the weather be very dirty, but not in any other case) he lies with his knees up, and the soles of his boots planted firmly on the cushion, so that if any low fellow should ask him to make room for a lady, he takes ample revenge upon her dress, without going at all out of his way to do it. He always sits with his hat on, and flourishes his stick in the air while the play is proceeding, with a dignified contempt of the performance; if it be possible for one or two out-and-out young gentlemen to get up a little crowding in the passages, they are quite in their element, squeezing, pushing, whooping, and shouting in the most humorous manner possible. If they can only succeed in irritating the gentleman who has a family of daughters under his charge, they are like to die with laughing, and boast of it among their companions for a week afterwards, adding, that one or two of them were "devilish fine girls," and that they really thought the youngest would have fainted, which was the only thing wanted to render the joke complete.

If the out-and-out young gentleman have a mother and sisters, of course he treats them with becoming contempt,

The Out-and-Out Young Gentleman

inasmuch as they (poor things!) having no notion of life or gaiety, are far too weak-spirited and moping for him. Sometimes, however, on a birth-day or at Christmas time, he cannot very well help accompanying them to a party at some old friend's, with which view he comes home when they have been dressed an hour or two, smelling very strongly of tobacco and spirits, and after exchanging his rough coat for some more suitable attire (in which however he loses nothing of the out-and-outer), gets into the coach and grumbles all the way at his own good-nature: his bitter reflections aggravated by the recollection, that Tom Smith has taken the chair at a little impromptu dinner at a fighting man's, and that a set-to was to take place on a dining-table, between the fighting man and his brother-in-law, which is probably "coming off" at that very instant.

As the out-and-out young gentleman is by no means at his ease in ladies' society, he shrinks into a corner of the drawing-room when they reach the friend's, and unless one of his sisters is kind enough to talk to him, remains there without being much troubled by the attentions of other people, until he espies, lingering outside the door, another gentleman, whom he at once knows, by his air and manner (for there is a kind of freemasonry in the craft) to be a brother out-and-outer, and towards whom he accordingly makes his way. Conversation being soon opened by some casual remark, the second out-and-outer confidentially informs the first that he is one of the rough sort and hates that kind of thing, only he couldn't very well be off coming; to which the other replies, that that's just his case—"and I'll tell you what," continues the out-and-outer, in a whisper, "I should like a glass of warm brandy and water just now,"—"Or a pint of stout and a pipe," suggests the other out-and-outer.

The discovery is at once made that they are sympathetic souls; each of them says at the same moment, that he sees the other understands what's what, and they become fast friends at once, more especially when it appears that the second out-and-outer is no other than a gentleman, long favourably known to his familiars as "Mr. Warmint Blake," who upon divers occasions has distinguished himself in a manner that would not have disgraced the fighting man, and who—having been a pretty long time about town—had the honour of once shaking hands with the celebrated Mr. Thurtell himself.

At supper, these gentlemen greatly distinguish themselves, brightening up very much when the ladies leave the table, and proclaiming aloud their intention of beginning to spend the evening—a process which is generally understood to be satisfactorily performed, when a great deal of wine is drunk and a great deal of noise made, both of which feats the out-and-out young gentlemen execute to perfection. Having protracted their sitting until long after the host and the other guests have adjourned to the drawing-room, and finding that they have drained the decanters empty, they follow them thither with complexions rather heightened, and faces rather bloated with wine; and the agitated lady of the house whispers her friends as they waltz together, to the great terror of the whole room, that "both Mr. Blake and Mr. Dummins are very nice sort of young men in their way, only they are eccentric persons, and unfortunately *rather too wild!*"

The remaining class of out-and-out young gentlemen is composed of persons who, having no money of their own, and a soul above earning any, enjoy similar pleasures, nobody knows how. These respectable gentlemen, without aiming quite so much at the out-and-out in external appearance, are distinguished by all the same amiable and attractive characteristics, in an equal or perhaps greater degree, and now and then find their way into society, through the medium of the other class of out-and-out young gentlemen, who will sometimes carry them home, and who usually pay their tavern bills. As they are equally gentlemanly, clever, witty, intelligent, wise, and well-bred, we need scarcely have recommended them to the peculiar consideration of the young ladies, if it were not that some of the gentle creatures whom we hold in such high respect, are perhaps a little too apt to confound a great many heavier terms with the light word eccentricity, which we beg them henceforth to take in a strictly Johnsonian sense, without any liberality or latitude of construction.

The Very Friendly Young Gentleman

—•—

We know—and all people know—so many specimens of this class, that in selecting the few heads our limits enable us to take from a great number, we have been induced to give the very friendly young gentleman the preference over many others, to whose claims upon a more cursory view of the question we had felt disposed to assign the priority.

The very friendly young gentleman is very friendly to everybody, but he attaches himself particularly to two, or at most to three, families; regulating his choice by their dinners, their circle of acquaintance, or some other criterion in which he has an immediate interest. He is of any age between twenty and forty, unmarried of course, must be fond of children, and is expected to make himself generally useful, if possible. Let us illustrate our meaning by an example, which is the shortest mode, and the clearest.

We encountered one day, by chance, an old friend of whom we had lost sight for some years, and who—expressing a strong anxiety to renew our former intimacy—urged us to dine with him on an early day, that we might talk over old times. We readily assented, adding, that we hoped we should be alone. "Oh, certainly, certainly," said our friend, "not a soul with us but Mincin." "And who is Mincin?" was our natural inquiry. "O don't mind him," replied our friend, "he's a most particular friend of mine, and a very friendly fellow you will find him;" and so he left us.

We thought no more about Mincin until we duly presented ourselves at the house next day, when, after a hearty welcome, our friend motioned towards a gentleman who had been previously showing his teeth by the fire-place, and gave us to understand that it was Mr. Mincin, of whom he had spoken. It required no great penetration on our part to discover at once that Mincin was in every respect a very friendly young gentleman.

"I am delighted," said Mincin, hastily advancing, and pressing our hand warmly between both of his, "I am delighted, I am sure, to make your acquaintance—(here he smiled)—very much delighted indeed—(here he exhibited a little emotion)—I assure you that I have looked forward to it anxiously for a very long time." Here he released our hands, and rubbing his own, observed that the day was severe, but that he was delighted to perceive from our appearance that it agreed with us wonderfully; and then went on to observe that, notwithstanding the coldness of the weather, he had that morning seen in the paper an exceedingly curious paragraph, to the effect, that there was now in the garden of Mr. Wilkins, of Chichester, a pumpkin measuring four feet in height, and eleven feet seven inches in circumference, which he looked upon as a very extraordinary piece of intelligence. We ventured to remark, that we had a dim recollection of having once or twice before observed a similar paragraph in the public prints; upon which Mr. Mincin took us confidentially by the button, and said, Exactly, exactly, to be sure, we were very right, and he wondered what the editors meant by putting in such things. Who the deuce, he should like to know, did they suppose cared about them? that struck him as being the best of it.

The lady of the house appeared shortly afterwards, and Mr. Mincin's friendliness, as will readily be supposed, suffered no diminution in consequence; he exerted much strength and skill in wheeling a large easy-chair up to the fire, and the lady being seated in it, carefully closed the door, stirred the fire, and looked to the windows to see that they admitted no air; having satisfied himself upon all these points, he expressed himself quite easy in his mind, and begged to know how she found herself to-day. Upon the lady's replying very well, Mr. Mincin (who it appeared was a medical gentleman) offered some general remarks upon the nature and treatment of colds in the head, which occupied us agreeably until dinner-time. During the meal, he devoted himself to complimenting everybody, not forgetting himself, so that we were an uncommonly agreeable quartette.

"I'll tell you what, Capper," said Mr. Mincin to our host, as he closed the room door after the lady had retired, "you have very great reason to be fond of your wife. Sweet woman, Mrs. Capper, sir!" "Nay, Mincin—I beg," interposed the host, as we were about to reply that Mrs. Capper unquestionably was particularly sweet—"Pray, Mincin, don't." "Why not?" exclaimed Mr. Mincin, "why not? Why should you feel any delicacy before your old friend—*our* old friend, if I may be allowed to call you so, sir; why should you, I ask?" We of course wished to know why he should also, upon which our friend admitted that Mrs. Capper *was* a very sweet woman, at which admission Mr. Mincin cried "Bravo!" and begged to propose Mrs. Capper with heartfelt enthusiasm, whereupon our host said, "Thank you, Mincin," with deep feeling; and gave us, in a low voice, to understand, that Mincin had saved Mrs. Capper's cousin's life no less than fourteen times in a year and a half, which he considered no common circumstance—an opinion to which we most cordially subscribed.

Now that we three were left to entertain ourselves with conversation, Mr. Mincin's extreme friendliness became every moment more apparent; he was so amazingly friendly, indeed, that it was impossible to talk about anything in which he had not the chief concern. We happened to allude to some affairs in which our friend and we had been mutually engaged nearly fourteen years before, when Mr. Mincin was all at once reminded of a joke which our friend had made on that day four years, which he positively must insist upon telling—and which he did tell accordingly, with many pleasant recollections of what he said, and what Mrs. Capper said, and how he well remembered that they had been to the play with orders on the very night previous, and had seen Romeo and Juliet, and the pantomime, and how Mrs. Capper being faint had been led into the lobby, where she smiled, said it was nothing after all, and went back again, with many other interesting and absorbing particulars: after which the friendly young gentleman went on to assure us, that our friend had experienced a marvellously prophetic opinion of that same pantomime, which was of such an admirable kind that two morning papers took the same view next day. To this our friend replied, with a little triumph, that in that instance he had some reason to think he had been correct, which gave the friendly young gentleman occasion to believe that our friend was always correct; and so we went on, until our friend, filling a bumper, said he must drink one glass to his dear friend Mincin, than whom he would say no man saved the lives of his acquaintances more, or had a more friendly heart. Finally, our friend having emptied his glass, said, "God bless you, Mincin,"—and Mr. Mincin and he shook hands across the table with much affection and earnestness.

But great as the friendly young gentleman is, in a limited scene like this, he plays the same part on a larger scale with increased *éclat*. Mr. Mincin is invited to an evening party with his dear friends the Martins, where he meets his dear friends the Cappers, and his dear friends the Watsons, and a hundred other dear friends too numerous to mention. He is as much at home with the Martins as with the Cappers; but how exquisitely he balances his attentions, and divides them among his dear friends! If he flirts with one of the Miss Watsons, he has one little Martin on the sofa pulling his hair, and the other little Martin on the carpet riding on his foot. He carries Mrs. Watson down to supper on one arm, and Miss Martin on the other, and takes wine so judiciously, and in such exact order, that it is impossible for the most punctilious old lady to consider herself neglected. If any young lady, being prevailed upon to sing, become nervous afterwards, Mr. Mincin leads her tenderly into the next room, and restores her with port wine, which she must take medicinally. If any gentleman be standing by the piano during the progress of the ballad, Mr. Mincin seizes him by the arm at one point of the melody, and softly beating time the while with his head, expresses in dumb show his intense perception of the delicacy of the passage. If anybody's self-love is to be flattered, Mr. Mincin is at hand. If anybody's overweening vanity is to be pampered, Mr. Mincin will surfeit it. What wonder that people of all stations and ages recognise Mr. Mincin's friendliness; that he is universally allowed to be handsome as amiable; that mothers think him an oracle, daughters a dear, brothers a beau, and fathers a wonder! And who would not have the reputation of the very friendly young gentleman?

THE MILITARY YOUNG GENTLEMAN

WE are rather at a loss to imagine how it has come to pass that military young gentlemen have obtained so much favour in the eyes of the young ladies of this kingdom. We cannot think so lightly of them as to suppose that the mere circumstance of a man's wearing a red coat ensures him a ready passport to their regard; and even if this were the case, it would be no satisfactory explanation of the circumstance, because, although the analogy may in some degree hold good in the case of mail coachmen and guards, still general postmen wear red coats, and *they* are not to our knowledge better received than other men; nor are firemen either, who wear (or used to wear) not only red coats but very resplendent and massive badges besides—much larger than epaulettes. Neither do the twopenny post-office boys, if the result of our inquiries be correct, find any peculiar favour in woman's eyes, although they wear very bright red jackets, and have the additional advantage of constantly appearing in public on horseback, which last circumstance may be naturally supposed to be greatly in their favour.

We have sometimes thought that this phenomenon may take its rise in the conventional behaviour of captains and colonels and other gentlemen in red coats on the stage, where they are invariably represented as fine swaggering fellows, talking of nothing but charming girls, their king and country, their honour and their debts, and crowing over the inferior classes of the community, whom they occasionally treat with a little gentlemanly swindling, no less to the improvement and pleasure of the audience, than to the satisfaction and approval of the choice spirits who consort with them. But we will not devote these pages to our speculations upon the subject, inasmuch as our business at the present moment is not so much with the young ladies who are bewitched by her Majesty's livery as with the young gentlemen whose heads are turned by it. For "heads" we had written "brains;" but upon consideration, we think the former the more appropriate word of the two.

These young gentlemen may be divided into two classes— young gentlemen who are actually in the army, and young gentlemen who, having an intense and enthusiastic admiration for all things appertaining to a military life, are compelled by adverse fortune or adverse relations to wear out their existence in some ignoble counting-house. We will take this latter description of military young gentlemen first.

The whole heart and soul of the military young gentleman are concentrated in his favourite topic. There is nothing that he is so learned upon as uniforms; he will tell you, without faltering for an instant, what the habiliments of any one regiment are turned up with; what regiment wear stripes down the outside and inside of the leg; and how many buttons the Tenth had on their coats; he knows to a fraction how many yards and odd inches of gold lace it takes to make an ensign in the Guards; is deeply read in the comparative merits of different bands, and the apparelling of trumpeters; and is very luminous indeed in descanting upon "crack regiments," and the "crack" gentlemen who compose them, of whose mightiness and grandeur he is never tired of telling.

We were suggesting to a military young gentleman only the other day, after he had related to us several dazzling instances of the profusion of half-a-dozen honourable ensign somebodies or nobodies in the articles of kid gloves and polished boots, that possibly "cracked" regiments would be an improvement upon "crack," as being a more expressive and appropriate designation, when he suddenly interrupted us by pulling out his watch, and observing that he must hurry off to the Park in a cab, or he would be too late to hear the band play. Not wishing to interfere with so important an engagement, and being in fact already slightly overwhelmed by the anecdotes of the honourable ensigns afore-mentioned, we made no attempt to detain the military young gentleman, but parted company with ready good-will.

Some three or four hours afterwards, we chanced to be walking down Whitehall, on the Admiralty side of the way, when, as we drew near to one of the little stone places in which a couple of horse-soldiers mount guard in the daytime, we were attracted by the motionless appearance and eager gaze of a young gentleman, who was devouring both man and horse with his eyes, so eagerly, that he seemed deaf and blind to all that was passing around him. We were not much surprised at the discovery that it was our friend, the military young gentleman, but we *were* a little astonished, when we returned from a walk to South Lambeth, to find him still there, looking on with the same intensity as before. As it was a very windy day, we felt bound to awaken the young gentleman from his reverie, when he inquired of us with great enthusiasm whether "that was not a glorious spectacle," and proceeded to give us a detailed account of the weight of every article of the spectacle's trappings, from the man's gloves to the horse's shoes.

We have made it a practice since, to take the Horse Guards in our daily walk, and we find it is the custom of military young gentlemen to plant themselves opposite the sentries and contemplate them at leisure, in periods varying from fifteen minutes to fifty, and averaging twenty-five. We were much struck a day or two since, by the behaviour of a very promising young butcher who (evincing an interest in the service, which cannot be too strongly commended or encouraged), after a prolonged inspection of the sentry, proceeded to handle his boots with great curiosity, and as much composure and indifference as if the man were wax-work.

But the really military young gentleman is waiting all this time, and at the very moment that an apology rises to our lips, he emerges from the barrack gate (he is quartered in a garrison town), and takes the way towards the high street. He wears

The Military Young Gentleman

his undress uniform, which somewhat mars the glory of his outward man; but still, how great, how grand, he is! What a happy mixture of ease and ferocity in his gait and carriage! and how lightly he carries that dreadful sword under his arm, making no more ado about it than if it were a silk umbrella! The lion is sleeping: only think, if an enemy were in sight, how soon he'd whip it out of the scabbard, and what a terrible fellow he would be!

But he walks on, thinking of nothing less than blood and slaughter; and now he comes in sight of three other military young gentlemen, arm-in-arm, who are bearing down towards him, clanking their iron heels on the pavement, and clashing their swords with a noise, which should cause all peaceful men to quail at heart. They stop to talk. See how the flaxen-haired young gentleman with the weak legs—he who has his pocket-handkerchief thrust into the breast of his coat—glares upon the faint-hearted civilians who linger to look upon his glory; how the next young gentleman elevates his head in the air, and majestically places his arms a-kimbo; while the third stands with his legs very wide apart, and clasps his hands behind him. Well may we inquire—not in familiar jest, but in respectful earnest—if you call that nothing? Oh, if some encroaching foreign power—the emperor of Russia, for instance, or any of those deep fellows— could only see those military young gentlemen, as they move on together towards the billiard-room over the way, wouldn't he tremble a little!

And then, at the theatre, at night, when the performances are by command of Colonel Fitz-Sordust and the officers of the garrison, what a splendid sight it is! How sternly the defenders of their country look round the house, as if in mute assurance to the audience, that they may make themselves comfortable regarding any foreign invasion, for they (the military young gentlemen) are keeping a sharp look-out, and are ready for anything. And what a contrast between them, and that stage-box full of grey-headed officers, with tokens of many battles about them, who have nothing at all in common with the military young gentlemen, and who—but for an old-fashioned kind of manly dignity in their looks and bearing—might be common hard-working soldiers, for anything they take the pains to announce to the contrary!

Ah! here is a family just come in, who recognise the flaxen-headed young gentleman; and the flaxen-headed young gentleman recognises them too, only he doesn't care to show it just now. Very well done indeed! He talks louder to the little group of military young gentlemen who are standing by him, and coughs to induce some ladies in the next box but one to look round, in order that their faces may undergo the same ordeal of criticism to which they have subjected, in not a wholly inaudible tone, the majority of the female portion of the audience. Oh! a gentleman in the same box looks round as if he were disposed to resent this as an impertinence; and the flaxen-headed young gentleman sees his friends at once, and hurries away to them with the most charming cordiality.

Three young ladies, one young man, and the mamma of the party, receive the military young gentleman with great warmth, and politeness, and in five minutes afterwards the military young gentleman, stimulated by the mamma, introduces the two other military young gentlemen with whom he was walking in the morning, who take their seats behind the young ladies and commence conversation; whereat the mamma bestows a triumphant bow upon a rival mamma, who has not succeeded in decoying any military young gentlemen, and prepares to consider her visitors, from that moment, three of the most elegant and superior young gentlemen in the whole world.

THE POLITICAL YOUNG GENTLEMAN

ONCE upon a time—*not* in the days when pigs drank wine, but in a more recent period of our history—it was customary to banish politics when ladies were present. If this usage still prevailed, we should have had no chapter for political young gentlemen, for ladies would have neither known nor cared what kind of monster a political young gentleman was. But as this good custom in common with many others, has "gone out," and left no word when it is likely to be home again; as political young ladies are by no means rare, and political young gentlemen the very reverse of scarce, we are bound in the strict discharge of our most responsible duty, not to neglect this natural division of our subject.

If the political young gentleman be resident in a country town (and there *are* political young gentlemen in country towns sometimes), he is wholly absorbed in his politics. As a pair of purple spectacles communicate the same uniform tint to all objects near and remote, so the political glasses with which the young gentleman assists his mental vision give to everything the hue and tinge of party feeling. The political young gentleman would as soon think of being struck with the beauty of a young lady in the opposite interest, as he would dream of marrying his sister to the opposite member.

If the political young gentleman be a Conservative, he has usually some vague ideas about Ireland and the Pope, which he cannot very clearly explain, but which he knows are the right sort of thing, and not to be very easily got over by the other side. He has also some choice sentences regarding church and state, culled from the banners in use at the last election, with which he intersperses his conversation at intervals with surprising effect. But his great topic is the constitution, upon which he will declaim, by the hour together, with much heat and fury; not that he has any particular information on the subject, but because he knows that the constitution is somehow church and state, and church and state somehow the constitution; and that the fellows on the other side say it isn't, which is quite a sufficient reason for him to say it is, and to stick to it.

Perhaps his greatest topic of all, though, is the people. If a fight takes place in a populous town, in which many noses are broken, and a few windows, the young gentleman throws down the newspaper with a triumphant air, and exclaims, "Here's your precious people!" if half-a-dozen boys run across the course at race time, when it ought to be kept clear, the young gentleman looks indignantly round, and begs you to observe the conduct of the people. If the gallery demand a hornpipe between the play and the afterpiece, the same young gentleman cries "No" and "Shame" till he is hoarse, and then inquires with a sneer what you think of popular moderation *now*. In short, the people form a never-failing theme for him; and when the attorney on the side of his candidate dwells upon it with great power of eloquence at election time, as he never fails to do, the young gentleman and his friends, and the body they head, cheer with great violence against *the other people*, with whom, of course, they have no possible connexion. In much the same manner the audience at a theatre never fail to be highly amused with any jokes at the expense of the public—always laughing heartily at some other public, and never at themselves.

If the political young gentleman be a Radical, he is usually a very profound person indeed, having great store of theoretical questions to put to you, with an infinite variety of possible cases and logical deductions therefrom. If he be of the utilitarian school, too, which is more than probable, he is particularly pleasant company, having many ingenious remarks to offer upon the voluntary principle, and various cheerful disquisitions connected with the population of the country, the position of Great Britain in the scale of nations, and the balance of power. Then he is exceedingly well versed in all doctrines of political economy, as laid down in the newspapers, and knows a great many parliamentary speeches by heart; nay, he has a small stock of aphorisms, none of them exceeding a couple of lines in length, which will settle the toughest question and leave you nothing to say. He gives all the young ladies to understand that Miss Martineau is the greatest woman that ever lived; and when they praise the good looks of Mr. Hawkins, the new member, says he's very well for a representative, all things considered, but he wants a little calling to account, and he is more than half afraid it will be necessary to bring him down on his knees for that vote on the miscellaneous estimates. At this the young ladies express much wonderment, and say surely a Member of Parliament is not to be brought upon his knees so easily; in reply to which the political young gentleman smiles sternly, and throws out dark hints regarding the speedy arrival of that day, when Members of Parliament will be paid salaries, and required to render weekly accounts of their proceedings; at which the young ladies utter many expressions of astonishment and incredulity, while their lady-mothers regard the prophecy as little else than blasphemous.

It is extremely improving and interesting, to hear two political young gentlemen, of diverse opinions, discuss some great question across a dinner-table; such as, whether, if the public were admitted to Westminster Abbey for nothing, they would or would not convey small chisels and hammers in their pockets, and immediately set about chipping all the noses off the statues; or whether, if they once got into the Tower for a shilling, they would not insist upon trying the crown on their own heads, and loading and firing off all the small arms in the armoury, to the great discomposure of Whitechapel and the Minories. Upon these, and many other momentous questions which agitate the public mind in these desperate days, they will discourse with great vehemence and irritation for a considerable time together, both leaving off precisely where they began, and each thoroughly persuaded that he has got the better of the other.

In society, at assemblies, balls, and playhouses, these political young gentlemen are perpetually on the watch for a political allusion, or anything which can be tortured or construed into being one; when, thrusting themselves into the very smallest openings for their favourite discourse, they fall upon the unhappy company tooth and nail. They have recently had many favourable opportunities of opening in churches, but as there the clergyman has it all his own way, and must not be contradicted, whatever politics he preaches, they are fain to hold their tongues until they reach the outer door, though at the imminent risk of bursting in the effort.

As such discussions can please nobody but the talkative parties concerned, we hope they will henceforth take the hint and discontinue them, otherwise we now give them warning, that the ladies have our advice to discountenance such talkers altogether.

THE DOMESTIC YOUNG GENTLEMAN

LET us make a slight sketch of our amiable friend, Mr. Felix Nixon. We are strongly disposed to think that, if we put him in this place, he will answer our purpose without another word of comment.

Felix, then, is a young gentleman who lives at home with his mother, just within the twopenny-post office circle of three miles from St. Martin-le-Grand. He wears India-rubber goloshes when the weather is at all damp, and always has a silk handkerchief neatly folded up in the right-hand pocket of his great-coat, to tie over his mouth when he goes home at night; moreover, being rather near-sighted, he carries spectacles for particular occasions, and has a weakish, tremulous voice, of which he makes great use, for he talks as much as any old lady breathing.

The two chief subjects of Felix's discourse, are himself and his mother, both of whom would appear to be very wonderful and interesting persons. As Felix and his mother are seldom apart in body, so Felix and his mother are scarcely ever separate in spirit. If you ask Felix how he finds himself to-day, he prefaces his reply with a long and minute bulletin of his mother's state of health; and the good lady in her turn, edifies her acquaintance with a circumstantial and alarming account: how he sneezed four times and coughed once, after being out in the rain the other night; but having his feet promptly put into hot water, and his head into a flannel-something, which we will not describe more particularly than by this delicate allusion, was happily brought round by the next morning, and enabled to go to business as usual.

Our friend is not a very adventurous or hot-headed person, but he has passed through many dangers, as his mother can testify: there is one great story in particular, concerning a hackney coachman who wanted to overcharge him one night for bringing them home from the play, upon which Felix gave the aforesaid coachman a look which his mother thought would have crushed him to the earth, but which did not crush him quite, for he continued to demand another sixpence, notwithstanding that Felix took out his pocket-book, and, with the aid of a flat candle, pointed out the fare in print, which the coachman obstinately disregarding, he shut the street door with a slam which his mother shudders to think of; and then, roused to the most appalling pitch of passion by the coachman knocking a double knock to show that he was by no means convinced, he broke with uncontrollable force from his parent and the servant girl, and running into the street without his hat, actually shook his fist at the coachman, and came back again with a face as white, Mrs. Nixon says, looking about her for a simile—as white as that ceiling. She never will forget his fury that night—never!

The Domestic Young Gentleman

To this account Felix listens with a solemn face, occasionally looking at you to see how it affects you; and, when his mother has made an end of it, adds that he looked at every coachman he met for three weeks afterwards, in hopes that he might see the scoundrel; whereupon Mrs. Nixon, with an exclamation of terror, requests to know what he would have done to him if he *had* seen him. At which Felix smiling darkly and clenching his right fist, she exclaims, "Goodness gracious!" with a distracted air, and insists upon extorting a promise that he never will on any account do anything so rash, which her dutiful son—it being something more than three years since the offence was committed—reluctantly concedes, and his mother, shaking her head prophetically, fears with a sigh that his spirit will lead him into something violent yet. The discourse then, by an easy transition, turns upon the spirit which glows within the bosom of Felix; upon which point Felix himself becomes eloquent, and relates a thrilling anecdote of the time when he used to sit up till two o'clock in the morning reading French, and how his mother used to say, "Felix, you will make yourself ill, I know you will;" and how *he* used to say, "Mother, I don't care—I will do it;" and how at last his mother privately procured a doctor to come and see him, who declared, the moment he felt his pulse, that if he had gone on reading one night more—only one night more—he must have put a blister on each temple, and another between his shoulders; and who, as it was, sat down upon the instant, and writing a prescription for a blue pill, said it must be taken immediately, or he wouldn't answer for the consequences. The recital of these and many other moving perils of the like nature, constantly harrows up the feelings of Mr. Nixon's friends.

Mrs. Nixon has a tolerably extensive circle of female acquaintance, being a good-humoured talkative, bustling little

The Domestic Young Gentleman

body, and to the unmarried girls among them she is constantly
vaunting the virtues of her son, hinting that she will be a very
happy person who wins him, but that they must mind their P's
and Q's, for he is very particular, and terribly severe upon
young ladies. At this last caution the young ladies resident in
the same row, who happen to be spending the evening there,
put their pocket-handkerchiefs before their mouths, and are
troubled with a short cough; just then Felix knocks at the door,
and his mother drawing the tea-table nearer the fire, calls out
to him, as he takes off his boots in the back parlour, that he
needn't mind coming in in his slippers, for there are only the
two Miss Greys and Miss Thompson, and she is quite sure they
will excuse *him*; and nodding to the two Miss Greys, she adds,
in a whisper, that Julia Thompson is a great favourite with
Felix; at which intelligence the short cough comes again, and
Miss Thompson in particular is greatly troubled with it, till
Felix coming in, very faint for want of his tea, changes the
subject of discourse, and enables her to laugh out boldly and
tell Amelia Grey not to be so foolish. Here they all three laugh,
and Mrs. Nixon says they are giddy girls; in which stage of the
proceedings, Felix, who has by this time refreshed himself with
the grateful herb that "cheers but not inebriates," removes his
cup from his countenance and says with a knowing smile, that
all girls are; whereat his admiring mama pats him on the back
and tells him not to be sly, which calls forth a general laugh
from the young ladies, and another smile from Felix, who
thinking he looks very sly indeed, is perfectly satisfied.

Tea being over, the young ladies resume their work, and
Felix insists upon holding a skein of silk while Miss Thompson
winds it on a card. This process having been performed to the
satisfaction of all parties, he brings down his flute in compliance

with a request from the youngest Miss Grey, and plays divers tunes out of a very small music-book till supper-time, when he is very facetious and talkative indeed. Finally, after half a tumblerful of warm sherry and water, he gallantly puts on his goloshes over his slippers, and telling Miss Thompson's servant to run on first and get the door open, escorts that young lady to her house, five doors off; the Miss Greys, who live in the next house but one, stopping to peep with merry faces from their own door till he comes back again, when they call out "Very well, Mr. Felix!" and trip into the passage with a laugh more musical than any flute that was ever played.

Felix is rather prim in his appearance, and perhaps a little priggish about his books and flute, and so forth, which have all their peculiar corners of peculiar shelves in his bed-room; indeed all his female acquaintance (and they are good judges) have long ago set him down as a thorough old bachelor. He is a favourite with them however, in a certain way, as an honest, inoffensive, kind-hearted creature; and as his peculiarities harm nobody, not even himself, we are induced to hope that many who are not personally acquainted with him will take our good word in his behalf, and be content to leave him to a long continuance of his harmless existence.

The Censorious Young Gentleman

—•—

There is an amiable kind of young gentleman going about in society, upon whom, after much experience of him, and considerable turning over of the subject in our mind, we feel it our duty to affix the above appellation. Young ladies mildly call him a "sarcastic" young gentleman, or a "severe" young gentleman. We, who know better, beg to acquaint them with the fact, that he is merely a censorious young gentleman, and nothing else.

The censorious young gentleman has the reputation among his familiars of a remarkably clever person, which he maintains by receiving all intelligence and expressing all opinions with a dubious sneer, accompanied with a half-smile, expressive of anything you please but good-humour. This sets people about thinking what on earth the censorious young gentleman means, and they speedily arrive at the conclusion that he means something very deep indeed; for they reason in this way—"This young gentleman looks so very knowing that he must mean something, and as I am by no means a dull individual, what a very deep meaning he must have if *I* can't find it out!" It is extraordinary how soon a censorious young gentleman may make a reputation in his own small circle if he bear this in his mind, and regulate his proceedings accordingly.

As young ladies are generally—not curious, but laudably desirous to acquire information, the censorious young gentleman is much talked about among them, and many surmises are hazarded regarding him. "I wonder," exclaims the eldest Miss Greenwood, laying down her work to turn up the lamp, "I wonder whether Mr. Fairfax will ever be married." "Bless me, dear," cries Miss Marshall, "whatever made you think of him?" "Really I hardly know," replies Miss Greenwood; "he is such a very mysterious person, that I often wonder about him." "Well, to tell you the truth," replies Miss Marshall, "and so do I." Here two other young ladies profess that they are constantly doing the like, and all present appear in the same condition except one young lady, who not scrupling to state that she considers Mr. Fairfax "a horror," draws down all the opposition of the others, which having been expressed in a great many ejaculatory passages, such as "Well, did I ever!" and "Lor, Emily, dear!" ma takes up the subject, and gravely states that she must say she does not think Mr. Fairfax by any means a horror, but rather takes him to be a young man of very great ability; "and I am quite sure," adds the worthy lady, "he always means a great deal more than he says."

The door opens at this point in the discourse, and who of all people alive walks into the room, but the very Mr. Fairfax, who has been the subject of conversation! "Well, it really is curious," cries ma, "we were at that very moment talking about you." "You did me great honour," replies Mr. Fairfax; "May I venture to ask what you were saying?" "Why, if you must know," returns the eldest girl, "we were remarking what a very mysterious man you are." "Ay, ay!" observes Mr. Fairfax, "indeed!" Now Mr. Fairfax says this ay, ay, and indeed, which are slight words enough in themselves, with so very unfathomable an air, and accompanies them with such a very equivocal smile, that ma and the young ladies are more than ever convinced that he means an immensity, and so tell him he is a very dangerous man, and seems to be always thinking ill of somebody, which is precisely the sort of character the censorious young gentleman is most desirous to establish; wherefore he says, "Oh, dear, no," in a tone, obviously intended to mean, "You have me there," and which gives him to understand that they have hit the right nail on the very centre of its head.

The Censorious Young Gentleman

When the conversation ranges from the mystery overhanging the censorious young gentleman's behaviour, to the general topics of the day, he sustains his character to admiration. He considers the new tragedy well enough *for* a new tragedy, but Lord bless us!—well, no matter; he could say a great deal on that point, but he would rather not, lest he should be thought ill-natured, as he knows he would be. "But is not Mr. So and So's performance truly charming?" inquires a young lady. "Charming!" replies the censorious young gentleman, "Oh, dear, yes, certainly; very charming—oh, very charming indeed." After this, he stirs the fire, smiling contemptuously all the while: and a modest young gentleman, who has been a silent listener, thinks what a great thing it must be to have such a critical judgment. Of music, pictures, books, and poetry, the censorious young gentleman has an equally fine conception. As to men and women, he can tell all about them at a glance. "Now let us hear your opinion of young Mrs. Barker," says some great believer in the powers of Mr. Fairfax, "but don't be too severe." "I never am severe," replies the censorious young gentleman. "Well, never mind that now. She is very lady-like, is she not?" "Lady-like!" repeats the censorious young gentleman (for he always repeats when he is at a loss for anything to say); "Did you observe her manner? Bless my heart and soul, Mrs. Thompson, did you observe her manner?—that's all I ask." "I thought I had done so," rejoins the poor lady, much perplexed; "I did not observe it very closely perhaps." "Oh, not very closely," rejoins the censorious young gentleman, triumphantly, "Very good; then *I* did. Let us talk no more about her." The censorious young gentleman purses up his lips, and nods his head sagely, as he says this; and it is forthwith whispered about that Mr. Fairfax (who, though he is a little prejudiced, must be admitted to be a very excellent judge) has observed something exceedingly odd in Mrs. Barker's manner.

ᴛʜᴇ ꜰᴜɴɴʏ ʏᴏᴜɴɢ ɢᴇɴᴛʟᴇᴍᴀɴ

As one funny young gentleman will serve as a sample of all funny young gentlemen, we purpose merely to note down the conduct and behaviour of an individual specimen of this class, whom we happened to meet at an annual family Christmas party in the course of this very last Christmas that ever came.

We were all seated round a blazing fire, which crackled pleasantly as the guests talked merrily and the urn steamed cheerily—for, being an old-fashioned party, there *was* an urn, and a teapot besides—when there came a postman's knock at the door, so violent and sudden, that it startled the whole circle, and actually caused two or three very interesting and most unaffected young ladies to scream aloud, and to exhibit many afflicting symptoms of terror and distress, until they had been several times assured by their respective adorers that they were in no danger. We were about to remark that it was surely beyond post-time, and must have been a runaway knock, when our host, who had hitherto been paralysed with wonder, sank into a chair in a perfect ecstasy of laughter, and offered to lay twenty pounds that it was that droll dog Griggins. He had no sooner said this, than the majority of the company and all the children of the house burst into a roar of laughter too, as if some inimitable joke flashed upon them simultaneously, and gave vent to various exclamations of— To be sure it must be Griggins, and How like him that was, and What spirits he was always in! with many other commendatory remarks of the like nature.

Not having the happiness to know Griggins, we became extremely desirous to see so pleasant a fellow, the more especially as a stout gentleman with a powdered head, who was sitting with his breeches buckles almost touching the hob, whispered us he was a wit of the first water,—when the door opened, and Mr. Griggins being announced, presented himself, amidst another shout of laughter and a loud clapping of hands from the younger branches. This welcome he acknowledged by sundry contortions of countenance, imitative of the clown in one of the new pantomimes, which were so extremely successful, that one stout gentleman rolled upon an ottoman in a paroxysm of delight, protesting, with many gasps, that if somebody didn't make that fellow Griggins leave off, he would be the death of him, he knew. At this the company only laughed more boisterously than before, and as we always like to accommodate our tone and spirit, if possible, to the humour of any society in which we find ourself, we laughed with the rest, and exclaimed, "Oh! capital, capital!" as loud as any of them.

When he had quite exhausted all beholders, Mr. Griggins received the welcomes and congratulations of the circle, and went through the needful introductions, with much ease and many puns. This ceremony over, he avowed his intention of sitting in somebody's lap unless the young ladies made room for him on the sofa, which being done, after a great deal of tittering

The Funny Young Gentleman

and pleasantry, he squeezed himself among them, and likened his condition to that of Love among the roses. At this novel jest we all roared once more. "You should consider yourself highly honoured, sir," said we. "Sir," replied Mr. Griggins, "you do me proud." Here everybody laughed again; and the stout gentleman by the fire whispered in our ear that Griggins was making a dead set at us.

The tea things having been removed, we all sat down to a round game, and here Mr. Griggins shone forth with peculiar brilliancy, abstracting other people's fish, and looking over their hands in the most comical manner. He made one most excellent joke in snuffing a candle, which was neither more nor less than setting fire to the hair of a pale young gentleman who sat next him, and afterwards begging his pardon with considerable humour. As the young gentleman could not see the joke however, possibly in consequence of its being on the top of his own head, it did not go off quite as well as it might have done; indeed, the young gentleman was heard to murmur some general references to "impertinence," and a "rascal," and to state the number of his lodgings in an angry tone—a turn of the conversation which might have been productive of slaughterous consequences, if a young lady, betrothed to the young gentleman, had not used her immediate influence to bring about a reconciliation: emphatically declaring in an agitated whisper, intended for his peculiar edification but audible to the whole table, that if he went on in that way, she never would think of him otherwise than as a friend, though as that she must always regard him. At this terrible threat the young gentleman became calm, and the young lady, overcome by the revulsion of feeling, instantaneously fainted.

Mr. Griggins's spirits were slightly depressed for a short period by this unlooked-for result of such a harmless pleasantry, but being promptly elevated by the attentions of the host and several glasses of wine, he soon recovered and became even more vivacious than before, insomuch that the stout gentleman previously referred to assured us that although he had known him since he was *that* high (something smaller than a nutmeg-grater), he had never beheld him in such excellent cue.

When the round game and several games at blind man's buff which followed it were all over, and we were going down to supper, the inexhaustible Mr. Griggins produced a small sprig of misletoe from his waistcoat pocket, and commenced a general kissing of the assembled females, which occasioned great commotion and much excitement. We observed that several young gentlemen—including the young gentleman with the pale countenance—were greatly scandalised at this indecorous proceeding, and talked very big among themselves in corners; and we observed too, that several young ladies, when remonstrated with by the aforesaid young gentlemen, called each other to witness how they had struggled, and protested vehemently that it was very rude, and that they were surprised at Mrs. Brown's allowing it, and that they couldn't bear it, and had no patience with such impertinence. But such is the gentle and forgiving nature of woman, that although we looked very narrowly for it, we could not detect the slightest harshness in the subsequent treatment of Mr. Griggins. Indeed, upon the whole, it struck us that among the ladies he seemed rather more popular than before!

To recount all the drollery of Mr. Griggins at supper, would fill such a tiny volume as this, to the very bottom of the outside cover. How he drank out of other people's glasses, and ate of other people's bread, how he frightened into screaming convulsions a little boy who was sitting up to supper in a high chair, by sinking below the table and suddenly reappearing with a mask on; how the hostess was really surprised that anybody could find a pleasure in tormenting children, and how the host frowned at the hostess, and felt convinced that Mr. Griggins had done it with the very best intentions; how Mr. Griggins explained, and how everybody's good-humour was restored but the child's;—to tell these and a hundred other things ever so briefly, would occupy more of our room and our readers' patience, than either they or we can conveniently spare. Therefore we change the subject, merely observing that we have offered no description of the funny young gentleman's personal appearance, believing that almost every society has a Griggins of its own, and leaving all readers to supply the deficiency, according to the particular circumstances of their particular case.

THE THEATRICAL YOUNG GENTLEMAN

—•—

ALL gentlemen who love the drama—and there are few gentleman who are not attached to the most intellectual and rational of all our amusements—do not come within this definition. As we have no mean relish for theatrical entertainments ourself, we are disinterestedly anxious that this should be perfectly understood.

The theatrical young gentleman has early and important information on all theatrical topics. "Well," says he, abruptly, when you meet him in the street, "here's a pretty to-do. Flimkins has thrown up his part in the melodrama at the Surrey."—"And what's to be done?" you inquire with as much gravity as you can counterfeit. "Ah, that's the point," replies the theatrical young gentleman, looking very serious; "Boozle declines it—positively declines it. From all I am told, I should say it was decidedly in Boozle's line, and that he would be very likely to make a great hit in it; but he objects on the ground of Flimkins having been put up in the part first, and says no earthly power shall induce him to take the character. It's a fine part, too—excellent business, I'm told. He has to kill six people in the course of the piece, and to fight over a bridge in red fire, which is as safe a card, you know, as can be. Don't mention it; but I hear that the last scene, when he is first poisoned, and then stabbed, by Mrs. Flimkins as Vengedora, will be the greatest thing that has been done these many years." With this piece of news, and laying his finger on his lips as a caution for you not to excite the town with it, the theatrical young gentleman hurries away.

The theatrical young gentleman, from often frequenting the different theatrical establishments, has pet and familiar names for them all. Thus Covent-Garden is the garden, Drury-Lane the lane, the Victoria the vic, and the Olympic the pic. Actresses, too, are always designated by their surnames only, as Taylor, Nisbett, Faucit, Honey; that talented and lady-like girl Sheriff, that clever little creature Horton, and so on. In the same manner he prefixes Christian names when he mentions the actors, as Charley Young, Jemmy Buckstone, Fred. Yates, Paul Bedford. When he is at a loss for a Christian name, the word "old" applied indiscriminately answers quite as well: as old Charley Mathews at Vestris's, old Harley, and old Braham. He has a great knowledge of the private proceedings of actresses, especially of their getting married, and can tell you in a breath half-a-dozen who have changed their names without avowing it. Whenever an alteration of this kind is made in the play-bills, he will remind you that he let you into the secret six months ago.

The theatrical young gentleman has a great reverence for all that is connected with the stage department of the different theatres. He would, at any time, prefer going a street or two out of his way, to omitting to pass a stage-entrance, into which he always looks with a curious and searching eye. If he can only identify a popular actor in the street, he is in a perfect transport of delight; and no sooner meets him, than he hurries back, and walks a few paces in front of him, so that he can turn round from time to time, and have a good stare at his features. He looks upon a theatrical-fund dinner as one of the most enchanting festivities ever known; and thinks that to be a member of the Garrick Club, and see so many actors in their plain clothes, must be one of the highest gratifications the world can bestow.

The theatrical young gentleman is a constant half-price visitor at one or other of the theatres, and has an infinite relish for all pieces which display the fullest resources of the establishment. He likes to place implicit reliance upon the play-bills when he goes to see a show-piece, and works himself up to such a pitch of enthusiasm, as not only to believe (if the bills say so) that there are three hundred and seventy-five people on the stage at one time in the last scene, but is highly indignant with you, unless you believe it also. He considers that if the stage be opened from the foot-lights to the back wall, in any new play, the piece is a triumph of dramatic writing, and applauds accordingly. He has a great notion of trap-doors too, and thinks any character going down or coming up a trap (no matter whether he be an angel or a demon—they both do it occasionally) one of the most interesting feats in the whole range of scenic illusion.

Besides these acquirements, he has several veracious accounts to communicate of the private manners and customs of different actors, which, during the pauses of a quadrille, he usually communicates to his partner, or imparts to his neighbour at a supper table. Thus he is advised, that Mr. Liston always had a footman in gorgeous livery waiting at the side-scene with a brandy-bottle and tumbler, to administer half a pint or so of spirit to him every time he came off, without which assistance he must infallibly have fainted. He knows for a fact, that, after an arduous part, Mr. George Bennett is put between two feather beds, to absorb the perspiration; and is credibly informed that Mr. Baker has for many years submitted to a course of lukewarm toast-and-water, to qualify him to sustain his favourite characters. He looks upon Mr. Fitz Ball as the principal dramatic genius and poet of the day, but holds that there are great writers extant besides him; in proof whereof, he refers you to various dramas and melo-dramas recently produced, of which he takes in all the sixpenny and three-penny editions as fast as they appear.

The theatrical young gentleman is a great advocate for violence of emotion and redundancy of action. If a father has to curse a child upon the stage, he likes to see it done in the thorough-going style, with no mistake about it: to which end it is essential that the child should follow the father on her knees, and be knocked violently over on her face by the old gentleman as he goes into a small cottage, and shuts the door behind him. He likes to see a blessing invoked upon the young lady, when the old gentleman repents, with equal earnestness, and accompanied by the usual conventional forms, which consist of the old gentleman looking anxiously up into the clouds, as if to see whether it rains, and then spreading an imaginary tablecloth in the air over the young lady's head— soft music playing all the while. Upon these, and other points of a similar kind, the theatrical young gentleman is a great critic indeed. He is likewise very acute in judging of natural expressions of the passions, and knows precisely the frown, wink, nod, or leer, which stands for any one of them, or the means by which it may be converted into any other: as jealousy, with a good stamp of the right foot, becomes anger; or wildness, with the hands clasped before the throat, instead of tearing the wig, is passionate love. If you venture to express a doubt of the accuracy of any of these portraitures, the theatrical young gentleman assures you, with a haughty smile, that it always has been done in that way, and he supposes they are not going to change it at this time of day to please you; to which, of course, you meekly reply that you suppose not.

There are innumerable disquisitions of this nature, in which the theatrical young gentleman is very profound— especially to ladies, whom he is most in the habit of entertaining with them; but as we have no space to recapitulate them at greater length, we must rest content with calling the attention of the young ladies in general to the theatrical young gentlemen of their own acquaintance.

THE POETICAL YOUNG GENTLEMAN

——•——

TIME was, and not very long ago either, when a singular epidemic raged among the young gentlemen, vast numbers of whom, under the influence of the malady, tore off their neckerchiefs, turned down their shirt-collars, and exhibited themselves in the open streets with bare throats and dejected countenances, before the eyes of an astonished public. These were poetical young gentlemen. The custom was gradually found to be inconvenient, as involving the necessity of too much clean linen and too large washing bills, and these outward symptoms have consequently passed away; but we are disposed to think, notwithstanding, that the number of poetical young gentlemen is considerably on the increase.

We know a poetical young gentleman—a very poetical young gentleman. We do not mean to say that he is troubled with the gift of poesy in any remarkable degree, but his countenance is of a plaintive and melancholy cast, his manner is abstracted and bespeaks affliction of soul: he seldom has his hair cut, and often talks about being an outcast and wanting a kindred spirit; from which, as well as from many general observations in which he is wont to indulge, concerning mysterious impulses, and yearnings of the heart, and the supremacy of intellect gilding all earthly things with the glowing magic of immortal verse, it is clear to all his friends that he has been stricken poetical.

The favourite attitude of the poetical young gentleman is lounging on a sofa with his eyes fixed upon the ceiling, or sitting bolt upright in a high-backed chair, staring with very round eyes at the opposite wall. When he is in one of these positions, his mother, who is a worthy affectionate old soul, will give you a nudge to bespeak your attention without disturbing the abstracted one, and whisper with a shake of the head, that John's imagination is at some extraordinary work or other, you may take her word for it. Hereupon John looks more fiercely intent upon vacancy than before, and suddenly snatching a pencil from his pocket, puts down three words and a cross on the back of a card, sighs deeply, paces once or twice across the room, inflicts a most unmerciful slap upon his head, and walks moodily up to his dormitory.

The poetical young gentleman is apt to acquire peculiar notions of things too, which plain, ordinary people, unblessed with a poetical obliquity of vision, would suppose to be rather distorted. For instance, when the sickening murder and mangling of a wretched woman was affording delicious food wherewithal to gorge the insatiable curiosity of the public, our friend the poetical young gentleman was in ecstasies—not of disgust, but admiration. "Heavens!" cried the poetical young gentleman, "how grand; how great!" We ventured deferentially to inquire upon whom these epithets were bestowed? our humble thoughts oscillating between the police officer who found the criminal, and the lock-keeper who found the head. "Upon whom!" exclaimed the poetical young gentleman in a frenzy of poetry, "Upon whom should they be bestowed but upon the murderer!"—and thereupon it came out, in a fine torrent of eloquence, that the murderer was a great spirit, a bold creature full of daring and nerve, a man of dauntless heart and determined courage, and withal a great casuist and able reasoner, as was fully demonstrated in his philosophical colloquies with the great and noble of the land. We held our

The Poetical Young Gentleman

peace, and meekly signified our indisposition to controvert these opinions—firstly, because we were no match at quotation for the poetical young gentleman; and secondly, because we felt it would be of little use our entering into any disputation if we were: being perfectly convinced that the respectable and immortal hero in question is not the first and will not be the last, hanged gentleman upon whom false sympathy or diseased curiosity will be plentifully expended.

This was a stern mystic flight of the poetical young gentleman. In his milder and softer moments he occasionally lays down his neckcloth, and pens stanzas, which sometimes find their way into a Lady's Magazine, or the "Poet's Corner" of some country newspaper; or which, in default of either vent for his genius, adorn the rainbow leaves of a lady's album. These are generally written upon some such occasions as contemplating the Bank of England by midnight, or beholding Saint Paul's in a snow-storm; and when these gloomy objects fail to afford him inspiration, he pours forth his soul in a touching address to a violet, or a plaintive lament that he is no longer a child, but has gradually grown up.

The poetical young gentleman is fond of quoting passages from his favourite authors, who are all of the gloomy and desponding school. He has a great deal to say too about the world, and is much given to opining, especially if he has taken anything strong to drink, that there is nothing in it worth living for. He gives you to understand, however, that for the sake of society, he means to bear his part in the tiresome play, manfully resisting the gratification of his own strong desire to make a premature exit; and consoles himself with the reflection that immortality has some chosen nook for himself and the other great spirits whom earth has chafed and wearied.

When the poetical young gentleman makes use of adjectives, they are all superlatives. Everything is of the grandest, greatest, noblest, mightiest, loftiest, or the lowest, meanest, obscurest, vilest, and most pitiful. He knows no medium, for enthusiasm is the soul of poetry; and who so enthusiastic as a poetical young gentleman? "Mr. Milkwash," says a young lady, as she unlocks her album to receive the young gentleman's original impromptu contribution, "how very silent you are! I think you must be in love." "Love!" cries the poetical young gentleman, starting from his seat by the fire and terrifying the cat, who scampers off at full speed, "Love! that burning, consuming passion; that ardour of the soul, that fierce glowing of the heart. Love! The withering, blighting influence of hope misplaced and affection slighted. Love did you say! Ha! ha! ha!"

With this, the poetical young gentleman laughs a laugh belonging only to poets and Mr. O. Smith of the Adelphi theatre, and sits down, pen in hand, to throw off a page or two of verse in the biting, semi-atheistical, demoniac style, which, like the poetical young gentleman himself, is full of sound and fury, signifying nothing.

𝕿HE "𝕿HROWING-OFF" 𝖄OUNG 𝕲ENTLEMAN

—•—

𝕿HERE is a certain kind of impostor—a bragging, vaunting, puffing young gentleman—against whom we are desirous to warn that fairer part of the creation, to whom we more peculiarly devote these our labours. And we are particularly induced to lay especial stress upon this division of our subject by a little dialogue we held some short time ago, with an esteemed young lady of our acquaintance, touching a most gross specimen of this class of men. We had been urging all the absurdities of his conduct and conversation, and dwelling upon the impossibilities he constantly recounted—to which indeed we had not scrupled to prefix a certain hard little word of one syllable and three letters—when our fair friend, unable to maintain the contest any longer, reluctantly cried, "Well; he certainly has a habit of throwing-off, but then—" "What then? Throw him off yourself," said we. And so she did, but not at our instance, for other reasons appeared, and it might have been better if she had done so at first.

The throwing-off young gentleman has so often a father possessed of vast property in some remote district of Ireland, that we look with some suspicion upon all young gentlemen who volunteer this description of themselves. The deceased grandfather of the throwing-off young gentleman was a man of immense possessions and untold wealth; the throwing-off young gentleman remembers, as well as if it were only yesterday, the deceased baronet's library, with its long rows of scarce and valuable books in superbly embossed bindings, arranged in cases reaching from the lofty ceiling to the oaken floor; and the fine antique chairs and tables; and the noble old castle of Ballykillbabaloo, with its splendid prospect of hill and dale, and wood, and rich wild scenery, and the fine hunting stables, and the spacious court-yards, "and—and—everything upon the same magnificent scale," says the throwing-off young gentleman, "princely; quite princely. Ah!" And he sighs as if mourning over the fallen fortunes of his noble house.

The throwing-off young gentleman is a universal genius; at walking, running, rowing, swimming, and skating he is unrivalled; at all games of chance or skill, at hunting, shooting, fishing, riding, driving, or amateur theatricals, no one can touch him—that is, *could* not, because he gives you carefully to understand, lest there should be any opportunity of testing his skill, that he is quite out of practice just now, and has been for some years. If you mention any beautiful girl of your common acquaintance in his hearing, the throwing-off young gentleman starts, smiles, and begs you not to mind him, for it was quite involuntary: people do say indeed that they were once engaged, but no—although she is a very fine girl, he was so situated at that time that he couldn't possibly encourage the—"but it's of no use talking about it!" he adds, interrupting himself; "she has got over it now, and I firmly hope and trust is happy." With this benevolent aspiration he nods his head in a mysterious manner, and whistling the first part of some popular air, thinks perhaps it will be better to change the subject.

There is another great characteristic of the throwing-off young gentleman, which is, that he "happens to be acquainted" with a most extraordinary variety of people in all parts of the world. Thus in all disputed questions, when the throwing-off young gentleman has no argument to bring forward, he invariably happens to be acquainted with some distant person intimately connected with the subject, whose testimony decides the point against you, to the great—may we say it?—to the great admiration of three young ladies out of every four, who consider the throwing-off young gentleman a very highly-connected young man, and a most charming person.

The "Throwing-off" Young Gentleman

Sometimes the throwing-off young gentleman happens to look in upon a little family circle of young ladies who are quietly spending the evening together, and then indeed is he at the very height and summit of his glory; for it is to be observed that he by no means shines to equal advantage in the presence of men as in the society of over-credulous young ladies, which is his proper element. It is delightful to hear the number of pretty things the throwing-off young gentleman gives utterance to, during tea, and still more so to observe the ease with which, from long practice and study, he delicately blends one compliment to a lady with two for himself. "Did you ever see a more lovely blue than this flower, Mr. Caveton?" asks a young lady who, truth to tell, is rather smitten with the throwing-off young gentleman. "Never," he replies, bending over the object of admiration, "never but in your eyes." "Oh, Mr. Caveton," cries the young lady, blushing of course. "Indeed I speak the truth," replies the throwing-off young gentleman, "I never saw any approach to them. I used to think my cousin's blue eyes lovely, but they grow dim and colourless beside yours." "Oh! a beautiful cousin, Mr. Caveton!" replies the young lady, with that perfect artlessness which is the distinguishing characteristic of all young ladies; "an affair, of course." "No; indeed, indeed you wrong me," rejoins the throwing-off young gentleman with great energy. "I fervently hope that her attachment towards me may be nothing but the natural result of our close intimacy in childhood, and that in change of scene, and among new faces, she may soon overcome it. *I* love her! Think not so meanly of me, Miss Lowfield, I beseech, as to suppose that title, lands, riches, and beauty, can influence *my* choice. The heart, the heart, Miss Lowfield." Here the throwing-off young gentleman sinks his voice to a still lower whisper; and the young lady duly proclaims to all the other young ladies, when they go up stairs to put their bonnets on, that Mr. Caveton's relations are all immensely rich, and that he is hopelessly beloved by title, lands, riches, and beauty.

We have seen a throwing-off young gentleman who, to our certain knowledge, was innocent of a note of music, and scarcely able to recognise a tune by ear, volunteer a Spanish air upon the guitar when he had previously satisfied himself that there was not such an instrument within a mile of the house.

We have heard another throwing-off young gentleman, after striking a note or two upon the piano, and accompanying it correctly (by dint of laborious practice) with his voice, assure a circle of wondering listeners that so acute was his ear that he was wholly unable to sing out of tune, let him try as he would. We have lived to witness the unmasking of another throwing-off young gentleman, who went out a-visiting in a military cap with a gold band and tassel, and who, after passing successfully for a captain and being lauded to the skies for his red whiskers, his bravery, his soldierly bearing, and his pride, turned out to be the dishonest son of an honest linen-draper in a small country town, and whom, if it were not for this fortunate exposure, we should not yet despair of encountering as the fortunate husband of some rich heiress. Ladies, ladies! the throwing-off young gentlemen are often swindlers, and always fools. So pray you avoid them.

THE YOUNG LADIES'
YOUNG GENTLEMAN

———•———

THIS young gentleman has several titles. Some young ladies consider him "a nice young man," others "a fine young man," others "quite a lady's man," others "a handsome man," others "a remarkably good-looking young man." With some young ladies he is "a perfect angel," and with others "quite a love." He is likewise a charming creature, a duck, and a dear.

The young ladies' young gentleman has usually a fresh colour and very white teeth, which latter articles, of course, he displays on every possible opportunity. He has brown or black hair, and whiskers of the same, if possible; but a slight tinge of red, or the hue which is vulgarly known as *sandy*, is not considered an objection. If his head and face be large, his nose prominent, and his figure square, he is an uncommonly fine young man, and worshipped accordingly. Should his whiskers meet beneath his chin, so much the better, though this is not absolutely insisted on; but he must wear an under-waistcoat, and smile constantly.

There was a great party got up by some party-loving friends of ours last summer, to go and dine in Epping Forest. As we hold that such wild expeditions should never be indulged in, save by people of the smallest means, who have no dinner at home, we should indubitably have excused ourself from attending, if we had not recollected that the projectors of the excursion were always accompanied on such occasions by a choice sample of the young ladies' young gentleman, whom we were very anxious to have an opportunity of meeting. This determined us, and we went.

We were to make for Chigwell in four glass coaches, each with a trifling company of six or eight inside, and a little boy belonging to the projectors on the box—and to start from the residence of the projectors, Woburn-place, Russell-square, at half-past ten precisely. We arrived at the place of rendezvous at the appointed time, and found the glass coaches and the little boys quite ready, and divers young ladies and young gentlemen looking anxiously over the breakfast-parlour blinds, who appeared by no means so much gratified by our approach as we might have expected, but evidently wished we had been somebody else. Observing that our arrival in lieu of the unknown occasioned some disappointment, we ventured to inquire who was yet to come, when we found from the hasty reply of a dozen voices, that it was no other than the young ladies' young gentleman.

"I cannot imagine," said the mama, "what has become of Mr. Balim—always so punctual, always so pleasant and agreeable. I am sure I can-*not* think." As these last words were uttered in that measured, emphatic manner which painfully announces that the speaker has not quite made up his or her mind what to say, but is determined to talk on nevertheless, the eldest daughter took up the subject, and hoped no accident had happened to Mr. Balim, upon which there was a general chorus of "Dear Mr. Balim!" and one young lady, more adventurous than the rest, proposed that an express should be straightway sent to dear Mr. Balim's lodgings. This, however, the papa resolutely opposed, observing, in what a short young lady behind us termed "quite a bearish way," that if Mr. Balim didn't choose to come, he might stop at home. At this all the daughters raised a murmur of "Oh pa!" except one sprightly little girl of eight or ten years old, who, taking advantage of a pause in the discourse, remarked, that perhaps Mr. Balim might have been married that morning—for which impertinent suggestion she was summarily ejected from the room by her eldest sister.

We were all in a state of great mortification and uneasiness, when one of the little boys, running into the room as airily as little boys usually run who have an unlimited allowance of animal food in the holidays, and keep their hands constantly forced down to the bottoms of very deep trouser-pockets when they take exercise, joyfully announced that Mr. Balim was at that moment coming up the street in a hackney-cab; and the intelligence was confirmed beyond all doubt a minute afterwards by the entry of Mr. Balim himself, who was received with repeated cries of "Where have you been, you naughty creature?" whereunto the naughty creature replied, that he had been in bed, in consequence of a late party the night before, and had only just risen. The acknowledgment awakened a variety of agonizing fears that he had taken no breakfast; which appearing after a slight cross-examination to be the real state of the case, breakfast for one was immediately ordered, notwithstanding Mr. Balim's repeated protestations that he couldn't think of it. He did think of it though, and thought better of it too, for he made a remarkably good meal when it came, and was assiduously served by a select knot of young ladies. It was quite delightful to see how he ate and drank, while one pair of fair hands poured out his coffee, and another put in the sugar, and another the milk; the rest of the company ever and anon casting angry glances at their watches, and the glass coaches,—and the little boys looking on in an agony of apprehension lest it should begin to rain before we set out: it might have rained all day, after we were once too far to turn back again, and welcome for aught they cared.

However, the cavalcade moved at length, every coachman being accommodated with a hamper between his legs something larger than a wheelbarrow; and the company being packed as closely as they possibly could in the carriages, "according," as one married lady observed, "to the immemorial custom, which was half the diversion of gipsy parties." Thinking it very likely it might be (we have never been able to discover the other half), we submitted to be stowed away with a cheerful aspect, and were fortunate enough to occupy one corner of a coach in which were one old lady, four young ladies, and the renowned Mr. Balim, the young ladies' young gentleman.

We were no sooner fairly off, than the young ladies' young gentleman hummed a fragment of an air, which induced a young lady to inquire whether he had danced to that the night before. "By Heaven, then, I did," replied the young gentleman, "and with a lovely heiress; a superb creature, with twenty thousand pounds." "You seem rather struck," observed another young lady. " 'Gad, she was a sweet creature," returned the young gentleman, arranging his hair. "Of course *she* was struck too?" inquired the first young lady. "How can you ask, love?" interposed the second; "Could she fail to be?" "Well, honestly, I think she was," observed the young gentleman. At this point of the dialogue, the young lady who had spoken first, and who sat on the young gentleman's right, struck him a severe blow on the arm with the rosebud, and said he was a vain man;

whereupon the young gentleman insisted on having the rosebud, and the young lady appealing for help to the other young ladies, a charming struggle ensued, terminating in the victory of the young gentleman, and the capture of the rosebud. This little skirmish over, the married lady, who was the mother of the rosebud, smiled sweetly upon the young gentleman, and accused him of being a flirt; the young gentleman pleading not guilty, a most interesting discussion took place upon the important point whether the young gentleman was a flirt or not, which being an agreeable conversation of a light kind, lasted a considerable time. At length, a short silence occurring, the young ladies on either side of the young gentleman fell suddenly fast asleep; and the young gentleman, winking upon us to preserve silence, won a pair of gloves from each, thereby causing them to wake with equal suddenness and to scream very loudly. The lively conversation to which this pleasantry gave rise, lasted for the remainder of the ride, and would have eked out a much longer one.

We dined rather more comfortably than people usually do under such circumstances, nothing having been left behind but the corkscrew and the bread. The married gentlemen were unusually thirsty, which they attributed to the heat of the weather; the little boys ate to inconvenience; mamas were very jovial, and their daughters very fascinating; and the attendants being well-behaved men, got exceedingly drunk at a respectful distance.

We had our eye on Mr. Balim at dinner-time, and perceived that he flourished wonderfully, being still surrounded by a little group of young ladies, who listened to him as an oracle, while he ate from their plates and drank from their glasses in a manner truly captivating from its excessive playfulness. His

The Young Ladies' Young Gentleman

conversation, too, was exceedingly brilliant. In fact, one elderly lady assured us that, in the course of a little lively *badinage* on the subject of ladies' dresses, he had evinced as much knowledge as if he had been born and bred a milliner.

As such of the fat people who did not happen to fall asleep after dinner entered upon a most vigorous game at ball, we slipped away alone into a thicker part of the wood, hoping to fall in with Mr. Balim, the greater part of the young people having dropped off in twos and threes, and the young ladies' young gentleman among them. Nor were we disappointed, for we had not walked far when, peeping through the trees, we discovered him before us, and truly it was a pleasant thing to contemplate his greatness.

The young ladies' young gentleman was seated upon the ground, at the feet of a few young ladies who were reclining on a bank; he was so profusely decked with scarfs, ribands, flowers, and other pretty spoils that he looked like a lamb—or perhaps a calf would be a better simile—adorned for the sacrifice. One young lady supported a parasol over his interesting head, another held his hat, and a third his neckcloth, which in romantic fashion he had thrown off; the young gentleman himself, with his hand upon his breast, and his face moulded into an expression of the most honeyed sweetness, was warbling forth some choice specimens of vocal music in praise of female loveliness, in a style so exquisitely perfect, that we burst into an involuntary shout of laughter, and made a hasty retreat.

What charming fellows these young ladies' young gentlemen are! Ducks, dears, loves, angels, are all terms inadequate to express their merit. They are such amazingly, uncommonly, wonderfully, nice men.

Conclusion

———•———

As we have placed before the young ladies so many specimens of young gentlemen, and have also in the dedication of this volume given them to understand how much we reverence and admire their numerous virtues and perfections; as we have given them such strong reasons to treat us with confidence, and to banish, in our case all that reserve and distrust of the male sex which, as a point of general behaviour, they cannot do better than preserve and maintain—we say, as we have done all this, we feel that now, when we have arrived at the close of our task, they may naturally press upon us the inquiry, what particular description of young gentlemen we can conscientiously recommend.

Here we are at a loss. We look over our list, and can neither recommend the bashful young gentleman, nor the out-and-out young gentleman, nor the very friendly young gentleman, nor the military young gentleman, nor the political young gentleman, nor the domestic young gentleman, nor the censorious young gentleman, nor the funny young gentleman, nor the theatrical young gentleman, nor the poetical young gentleman, nor the throwing-off young gentleman, nor the young ladies' young gentleman.

As there are some good points about many of them, which still are not sufficiently numerous to render any one among them eligible, as a whole, our respectful advice to the young ladies is, to seek for a young gentleman who unites in himself the best qualities of all, and the worst weaknesses of none, and lead him forthwith to the hymeneal altar, whether he will or no. And to the young lady who secures him, we beg to tender one short fragment of matrimonial advice, selected from many sound passages of a similar tendency, to be found in a letter written by Dean Swift to a young lady on her marriage.

"The grand affair of your life will be, to gain and preserve the esteem of your husband. Neither good-nature nor virtue will suffer him to *esteem* you against his judgment; and although he is not capable of using you ill, yet you will in time grow a thing indifferent and perhaps contemptible, unless you can supply the loss of youth and beauty with more durable qualities. You have but a very few years to be young and handsome in the eyes of the world; and as few months to be so in the eyes of a husband who is not a fool; for I hope you do not still dream of charms and raptures, which marriage ever did, and ever will, put a sudden end to."

From the anxiety we express for the proper behaviour of the fortunate lady after marriage, it may possibly be inferred that the young gentleman to whom we have so delicately alluded, is no other than ourself. Without in any way committing ourself upon this point, we have merely to observe, that we are ready to receive sealed offers containing a full specification of age, temper, appearance, and condition; but we beg it to be distinctly understood that we do not pledge ourself to accept the highest bidder.

These offers may be forwarded to the Publishers, Messrs. Chapman and Hall, one hundred and eighty-six, Strand, London; to whom all pieces of plate and other testimonials of approbation from the young ladies generally, are respectfully requested to be addressed.

SKETCHES
OF
YOUNG
COUPLES

Sketches

OF

Young Couples;

WITH AN

URGENT REMONSTRANCE TO THE GENTLEMEN OF
ENGLAND

(BEING BACHELORS OR WIDOWERS),

ON THE PRESENT ALARMING CRISIS.

———•———

BY THE AUTHOR OF
"SKETCHES OF YOUNG GENTLEMEN."

———•———

WITH SIX ILLUSTRATIONS

BY

"PHIZ."

An Urgent Remonstrance, &c.

TO THE GENTLEMEN OF ENGLAND,

(BEING BACHELORS OR WIDOWERS,)

THE REMONSTRANCE OF THEIR FAITHFUL FELLOW-SUBJECT,

SHEWETH,—

THAT Her Most Gracious Majesty, Victoria, by the Grace of God of the United Kingdom of Great Britain and Ireland Queen, Defender of the Faith, did, on the 23rd day of November last past, declare and pronounce to Her Most Honourable Privy Council, Her Majesty's Most Gracious intention of entering into the bonds of wedlock.

THAT her Most Gracious Majesty, in so making known Her Most Gracious intention to Her Most Honourable Privy Council as aforesaid, did use and employ the words—"It is my intention to ally myself in marriage with Prince Albert of Saxe Coburg and Gotha."

THAT the present is Bissextile, or Leap Year, in which it is held and considered lawful for any lady to offer and submit proposals of marriage to any gentleman, and to enforce and insist upon acceptance of the same, under pain of a certain fine or penalty; to wit, one silk or satin dress of the first quality, to be chosen by the lady and paid (or owed) for, by the gentleman.

THAT these and other the horrors and dangers with which the said Bissextile, or Leap Year, threatens the gentlemen of

England on every occasion of its periodical return, have been greatly aggravated and augmented by the terms of Her Majesty's said Most Gracious communication, which have filled the heads of divers young ladies in this Realm with certain new ideas destructive to the peace of mankind, that never entered their imagination before.

THAT a case has occurred in Camberwell, in which a young lady informed her Papa that "she intended to ally herself in marriage" with Mr. Smith of Stepney; and that another, and a very distressing case, has occurred at Tottenham, in which a young lady not only stated her intention of allying herself in marriage with her cousin John, but, taking violent possession of her said cousin, actually married him.

THAT similar outrages are of constant occurrence, not only in the capital and its neighbourhood, but throughout the kingdom, and that unless the excited female populace be speedily checked and restrained in their lawless proceedings, most deplorable results must ensue therefrom; among which may be anticipated a most alarming increase in the population of the country, with which no efforts of the agricultural or manufacturing interest can possibly keep pace.

THAT there is strong reason to suspect the existence of a most extensive plot, conspiracy, or design, secretly contrived by vast numbers of single ladies in the United Kingdom of Great Britain and Ireland, and now extending its ramifications in every quarter of the land; the object and intent of which plainly appears to be the holding and solemnising of an enormous and unprecedented number of marriages, on the day on which the nuptials of Her said Most Gracious Majesty are performed.

An Urgent Remonstrance, &c.

THAT such plot, conspiracy, or design, strongly savours of Popery, as tending to the discomfiture of the Clergy of the Established Church, by entailing upon them great mental and physical exhaustion; and that such Popish plots are fomented and encouraged by Her Majesty's Ministers, which clearly appears—not only from Her Majesty's principal Secretary of State for Foreign Affairs traitorously getting married while holding office under the Crown; but from Mr. O'Connell having been heard to declare and avow that, if he had a daughter to marry, she should be married on the same day as Her said Most Gracious Majesty.

THAT such arch plots, conspiracies, and designs, besides being fraught with danger to the Established Church, and (consequently) to the State, cannot fail to bring ruin and bankruptcy upon a large class of Her Majesty's subjects; as a great and sudden increase in the number of married men occasioning the comparative desertion (for a time) of Taverns, Hotels, Billiard-rooms, and Gaming-Houses, will deprive the Proprietors of their accustomed profits and returns. And in further proof of the depth and baseness of such designs, it may be here observed, that all proprietors of Taverns, Hotels, Billiard-rooms, and Gaming-Houses, are (especially the last) uniformly devoted to the Protestant religion.

———◆———

FOR all these reasons, and many others of no less gravity and import, an urgent appeal is made to the gentlemen of England (being bachelors or widowers) to take immediate steps for convening a Public meeting; To consider of the best and surest means of averting the dangers with which they are threatened by the recurrence of Bissextile, or Leap Year, and the additional sensation created among single ladies by the terms of Her Majesty's most Gracious Declaration; To take measures, without delay, for resisting the said single Ladies, and counteracting their evil designs; And to pray Her Majesty to dismiss her present Ministers, and to summon to her Councils those distinguished Gentlemen in various Honourable Professions who, by insulting on all occasions the only Lady in England who can be insulted with safety, have given a sufficient guarantee to Her Majesty's Loving Subjects that they, at least, are qualified to make war with women, and are already expert in the use of those weapons which are common to the lowest and most abandoned of the sex.

CONTENTS

———•———

LIST OF ILLUSTRATIONS

———•———

THE YOUNG COUPLE

·

THERE is to be a wedding this morning at the corner house in the terrace. The pastry-cook's people have been there half-a-dozen times already; all day yesterday there was a great stir and bustle, and they were up this morning as soon as it was light. Miss Emma Fielding is going to be married to young Mr. Harvey.

Heaven alone can tell in what bright colours this marriage is painted upon the mind of the little housemaid at number six, who has hardly slept a wink all night with thinking of it, and now stands on the unswept door-steps leaning upon her broom, and looking wistfully towards the enchanted house. Nothing short of omniscience can divine what visions of the baker, or the green-grocer, or the smart and most insinuating butterman, are flitting across her mind—what thoughts of how she would dress on such an occasion, if she were a lady—of how she would dress, if she were only a bride—of how cook would dress, being bridesmaid, conjointly with her sister "in place" at Fulham, and how the clergyman, deeming them so many ladies, would be quite humbled and respectful. What day-dreams of hope and happiness—of life being one perpetual holiday, with no master and no mistress to grant or withhold it—of every Sunday being a Sunday out—of pure freedom as to curls and ringlets, and no obligation to hide fine heads of hair in caps—what pictures of happiness, vast and immense to her, but utterly ridiculous to us, bewilder the brain of the little housemaid at number six, all called into existence by the wedding at the corner!

We smile at such things, and so we should, though perhaps for a better reason than commonly presents itself. It should be pleasant to us to know that there are notions of happiness so moderate and limited, since upon those who entertain them, happiness and lightness of heart are very easily bestowed.

But the little housemaid is awakened from her reverie, for forth from the door of the magical corner house there runs towards her, all fluttering in smart new dress and streaming ribands, her friend Jane Adams, who comes all out of breath to redeem a solemn promise of taking her in, under cover of the confusion, to see the breakfast table spread forth in state, and—sight of sights!—her young mistress ready dressed for church.

And there, in good truth, when they have stolen up stairs on tiptoe and edged themselves in at the chamber-door—there is Miss Emma "looking like the sweetest picter," in a white chip bonnet and orange-flower, and all other elegancies becoming a bride (with the make, shape, and quality of every article of which the girl is perfectly familiar in one moment, and never forgets to her dying day)—and there is Miss Emma's mamma in tears, and Miss Emma's papa comforting her, and saying how that of course she has been long looking forward to this, and how happy she ought to be; and there too is Miss Emma's sister with her arms round her neck, and the other bridesmaid, all smiles and tears, quieting the children, who would cry more but that they are so finely dressed, and yet sob for fear sister Emma should be taken away—and it is all so affecting, that the two servant-girls cry more than anybody; and Jane Adams, sitting down upon the stairs, when they have crept away, declares that her legs tremble so that she don't know what to do, and that she will say for Miss Emma, that she never had a hasty word from her, and that she does hope and pray she may be happy.

But Jane soon comes round again, and then surely there never was anything like the breakfast table, glittering with plate and china, and set out with flowers and sweets, and long-necked bottles, in the most sumptuous and dazzling manner. In the centre, too, is the mighty charm, the cake, glistening with frosted sugar, and garnished beautifully. They agree that there ought to be a little Cupid under one of the barley-sugar temples, or at least two hearts and an arrow; but, with this exception, there is nothing to wish for, and a table could not be handsomer. As they arrive at this conclusion, who should come in but Mr. John! To whom Jane says that it's only Anne from number six; and John says *he* knows, for he's often winked his eye down the area, which causes Anne to blush and look confused. She is going away, indeed; when Mr. John will have it that she must drink a glass of wine, and he say, Never mind it's being early in the morning, it won't hurt her: so they shut the door and pour out the wine; and Anne drinking Jane's health, and adding, "and here's wishing you yours, Mr. John," drinks it in a great many sips,—Mr. John all the time making jokes appropriate to the occasion. At last Mr. John, who has waxed bolder by degrees, pleads the usage at weddings, and claims the privilege of a kiss, which he obtains after a great scuffle; and footsteps being now heard on the stairs, they disperse suddenly.

By this time a carriage has driven up to convey the bride to church, and Anne of number six prolonging the process of "cleaning her door," has the satisfaction of beholding the bride and bridesmaids, and the papa and mamma, hurry into the same and drive rapidly off. Nor is this all, for soon other carriages begin to arrive with a *posse* of company all beautifully dressed, at whom she could stand and gaze for ever; but having something else to do, is compelled to take one last long look and shut the street-door.

And now the company have gone down to breakfast, and tears have given place to smiles, for all the corks are out of the long-necked bottles, and their contents are disappearing rapidly. Miss Emma's papa is at the top of the table; Miss Emma's mamma at the bottom; and beside the latter are Miss Emma herself and her husband,—admitted on all hands to be the handsomest and most interesting young couple ever known. All down both sides of the table, too, are various young ladies, beautiful to see, and various young gentlemen who seem to think so; and there, in a post of honour, is an unmarried aunt of Miss Emma's, reported to possess unheard-of riches, and to have expressed vast testamentary intentions respecting her favourite niece and new nephew. This lady has been very liberal and generous already, as the jewels worn by the bride abundantly testify, but that is nothing to what she means to do, or even to what she has done, for she put herself in close communication with the dressmaker three months ago, and prepared a wardrobe (with some articles worked by her own hands) fit for a princess. People may call her an old maid, and so she may be, but she is neither cross nor ugly for all that; on the contrary, she is very cheerful and pleasant-looking, and very kind and tender-hearted; which is no matter of surprise except to those who yield to popular prejudices without thinking why, and will never grow wiser and never know better.

Of all the company though, none are more pleasant to behold or better pleased with themselves than two young children, who in honour of the day, have seats among the guests. Of these, one is a little fellow of six or eight years old, brother to the bride,—and the other a girl of the same age, or something younger, whom he calls "his wife." The real bride and bridegroom are not more devoted than they: he all love and attention, and she all blushes and fondness, toying with a little bouquet which he gave her this morning, and placing the scattered rose-leaves in her bosom with nature's own coquettishness. They have dreamt of each other in their quiet dreams, these children, and their little hearts have been nearly broken when the absent one has been dispraised in jest. When will there come in after life a passion so earnest, generous, and true as theirs; what, even in its gentlest realities, can have the grace and charm that hover round such fairy lovers!

By this time the merriment and happiness of the feast have gained their height; certain ominous looks begin to be exchanged between the bridesmaids, and somehow it gets whispered about that the carriage which is to take the young couple into the country has arrived. Such members of the party as are most disposed to prolong its enjoyments, affect to consider this a false alarm, but it turns out too true, being speedily confirmed, first by the retirement of the bride and a select file of intimates who are to prepare her for the journey, and secondly by the withdrawal of the ladies generally. To this there ensues a particularly awkward pause, in which everybody essays to be facetious, and nobody succeeds; at length the bridegroom makes a mysterious disappearance in obedience to some equally mysterious signal; and the table is deserted.

Now, for at least six weeks last past it has been solemnly devised and settled that the young couple should go away in secret; but they no sooner appear without the door than the

Departure of the Young Couple

drawing-room windows are blocked up with ladies waving their handkerchiefs and kissing their hands, and the dining-room panes with gentlemen's faces beaming farewell in every queer variety of its expression. The hall and steps are crowded with servants in white favours, mixed up with particular friends and relations who have darted out to say good-bye; and foremost in the group are the tiny lovers arm in arm, thinking, with fluttering hearts, what happiness it would be to dash away together in that gallant coach, and never part again.

The bride has barely time for one hurried glance at her old home, when the steps rattle, the door slams, the horses clatter on the pavement, and they have left it far away.

A knot of women servants still remain clustered in the hall, whispering among themselves, and there of course is Anne from number six, who has made another escape on some plea or other, and been an admiring witness of the departure. There are two points on which Anne expatiates over and over again, without the smallest appearance of fatigue, or intending to leave off; one is, that she "never see in all her life such a—oh such a angel of a gentleman as Mr. Harvey"—and the other, that she "can't tell how it is, but it don't seem a bit like a work-a-day, or a Sunday neither—it's all so unsettled and unregular."

𝕿HE 𝕵ORMAL 𝕮OUPLE

———◆———

𝕿HE formal couple are the most prim, cold, immovable, and unsatisfactory people on the face of the earth. Their faces, voices, dress, house, furniture, walk, and manner, are all the essence of formality, unrelieved by one redeeming touch of frankness, heartiness, or nature.

Everything with the formal couple resolves itself into a matter of form. They don't call upon you on your account, but their own; not to see how you are, but to show how they are: it is not a ceremony to do honour to you, but to themselves,—not due to your position, but to theirs. If one of a friend's children die, the formal couple are as sure and punctual in sending to the house as the undertaker; if a friend's family be increased, the monthly nurse is not more attentive than they. The formal couple, in fact, joyfully seize all occasions of testifying their good-breeding and precise observance of the little usages of society; and for you, who are the means to this end, they care as much as a man does for the tailor who has enabled him to cut a figure or a woman for the milliner who has assisted her to conquest.

Having an extensive connexion among that kind of people who make acquaintances and eschew friends, the formal gentleman attends from time to time a great many funerals, to which he is formally invited, and to which he formally goes, as returning a call for the last time. Here his deportment is of the most faultless description; he knows the exact pitch of voice it is proper to assume, the sombre look he ought to wear, the melancholy tread which should be his gait for the day. He is perfectly acquainted with all the dreary courtesies to be observed in the mourning coach; knows when to sigh, and when he hides his nose in the white handkerchief; and looks into the grave and shakes his head when the ceremony is concluded, with the sad formality of a mute.

"What kind of funeral was it?" says the formal lady, when he returns home. "Oh!" replies the formal gentleman, "there never was such a gross and disgusting impropriety; there were no feathers!" "No feathers!" cries the lady, as if on wings of black feathers dead people fly to Heaven, and lacking them, they must of necessity go elsewhere. Her husband shakes his head; and further adds, that they had seed-cake instead of plum-cake, and that it was all white wine. "All white wine!" exclaims his wife. "Nothing but sherry and madeira," says the husband. "What! no port?" "Not a drop." No port, no plums, and no feathers! "You will recollect, my dear," says the formal lady, in a voice of stately reproof, "that when we first met this poor man who is now dead and gone, and he took the very strange course of addressing me at dinner without being previously introduced, I ventured to express my opinion that the family were quite ignorant of etiquette, and very imperfectly acquainted with the decencies of life. You have now had a sad opportunity of judging for yourself, and all I have to say is, that I trust you will never go to a funeral *there* again." "My dear," replies the formal gentleman, "I never will." So the informal deceased is cut in his grave; and the formal couple, when they tell the story of the funeral, shake their heads, and wonder what some people's feelings *are* made of, and what their notions of propriety *can* be!

If the formal couple have a family (which they sometimes have), they are not children, but little, pale, sour, sharp-nosed men and women; and so exquisitely brought up, that they might be very old dwarfs for anything that appeareth to the contrary. Indeed, they are so acquainted with forms and conventionalities, and conduct themselves with such strict decorum, that to see the little girl break a looking-glass in some wild outbreak, or the little boy kick his parents, would be to any visitor an unspeakable relief and consolation.

The formal couple are always sticklers for what is rigidly proper, and have a great readiness in detecting hidden impropriety of speech or thought, which by less scrupulous people would be wholly unsuspected. Thus, if they pay a visit to the theatre, they sit all night in a perfect agony lest anything improper or immoral should proceed from the stage; and if anything should happen to be said which admits of a double construction, they never fail to take it up directly, and to express by their looks the great outrage which their feelings have sustained. Perhaps this is their chief reason for absenting themselves almost entirely from places of public amusement. They go sometimes to the Exhibition of the Royal Academy;—but that is often more shocking than the stage itself, and the formal lady thinks that it really is high time Mr. Etty was prosecuted and made a public example of.

We made one at a christening party not long since, where there were amongst the guests a formal couple, who suffered the acutest torture from certain jokes, incidental to such an occasion, cut—and very likely dried also—by one of the godfathers; a red-faced elderly gentleman, who, being highly popular with the rest of the company, had it all his own way, and was in great spirits. It was at supper-time that this gentleman came out in full force. We—being of a grave and quiet demeanour—had been chosen to escort the formal lady down stairs, and, sitting beside her, had a favourable opportunity of observing her emotions.

We have a shrewd suspicion that, in the very beginning, and in the first blush—literally the first blush—of the matter, the formal lady had not felt quite certain whether the being present at such a ceremony, and encouraging, as it were, the public exhibition of a baby, was not an act involving some degree of indelicacy and impropriety; but certain we are, that when that baby's health was drunk, and allusions were made, by a grey-headed gentleman proposing it, to the time when he had dandled in his arms the young Christian's mother,—certain we are that then the formal lady took the alarm, and recoiled from the old gentleman as from a hoary profligate. Still she bore it; she fanned herself with an indignant air, but still she bore it. A comic song was sung, involving a confession from some imaginary gentleman that he had kissed a female, and yet the formal lady bore it. But when at last, the health of the godfather before mentioned being drunk, the godfather rose to return thanks, and in the course of his observations darkly hinted at babies yet unborn, and even contemplated the possibility of the subject of that festival having brothers and sisters, the formal lady could endure no more, but, bowing slightly round, and sweeping haughtily past the offender, left the room in tears, under the protection of the formal gentleman.

₢HE ₤OVING ₡OUPLE

—◆—

₢HERE cannot be a better practical illustration of the wise saw and ancient instance, that there may be too much of a good thing, than is presented by a loving couple. Undoubtedly it is meet and proper that two persons joined together in holy matrimony should be loving, and unquestionably it is pleasant to know and see that they are so; but there is a time for all things, and the couple who happen to be always in a loving state before company, are well nigh intolerable.

And in taking up this position we would have it distinctly understood that we do not seek alone the sympathy of bachelors, in whose objection to loving couples we recognise interested motives and personal considerations. We grant that to that unfortunate class of society there may be something very irritating, tantalising, and provoking, in being compelled to witness those gentle endearments and chaste interchanges which to loving couples are quite the ordinary business of life. But while we recognise the natural character of the prejudice to which these unhappy men are subject, we can neither receive their biassed evidence, nor address ourself to their inflamed and angered minds. Dispassionate experience is our only guide; and in these moral essays we seek no less to reform hymeneal offenders than to hold out a timely warning to all rising couples, and even to those who have not yet set forth upon their pilgrimage towards the matrimonial altar.

Let all couples, present or to come, therefore profit by the example of Mr. and Mrs. Leaver, themselves a loving couple in the first degree.

Mr. and Mrs. Leaver are pronounced by Mrs. Starling, a widow lady who lost her husband when she was young, and lost herself about the same time—for by her own count she has never since grown five years older—to be a perfect model of wedded felicity. "You would suppose," says the romantic lady, "that they were lovers only just now engaged. Never was such happiness! They are so tender, so affectionate, so attached to each other, so enamoured, that positively nothing can be more charming!"

"Augusta, my soul," says Mr. Leaver. "Augustus, my life," replies Mrs. Leaver. "Sing some little ballad, darling," quoth

The Loving Couple

Mr. Leaver. "I couldn't, indeed, dearest," returns Mrs. Leaver. "Do, my dove," says Mr. Leaver. "I couldn't possibly, my love," replies Mrs. Leaver; "and it's very naughty of you to ask me." "Naughty, darling!" cries Mr. Leaver. "Yes, very naughty, and very cruel," returns Mrs. Leaver, "for you know I have a sore throat, and that to sing would give me great pain. You're a monster, and I hate you. Go away!" Mrs. Leaver has said "Go away," because Mr. Leaver has tapped her under the chin: Mr. Leaver not doing as he is bid, but on the contrary, sitting down beside her, Mrs. Leaver slaps Mr. Leaver; and Mr. Leaver in return slaps Mrs. Leaver, and it being now time for all persons present to look the other way, they look the other way, and hear a still small sound as of kissing, at which Mrs. Starling is thoroughly enraptured, and whispers her neighbour that if all married couples were like that, what a heaven this earth would be!

The loving couple are at home when this occurs, and maybe only three or four friends are present, but, unaccustomed to reserve upon this interesting point, they are pretty much the same abroad. Indeed upon some occasions, such as a pic-nic or a water-party, their lovingness is even more developed, as we had an opportunity last summer of observing in person.

There was a great water-party made up to go to Twickenham and dine, and afterwards dance in an empty villa by the river-side, hired expressly for the purpose. Mr. and Mrs. Leaver were of the company; and it was our fortune to have a seat in the same boat, which was an eight-oared galley, manned by amateurs, with a blue striped awning of the same pattern as their Guernsey shirts, and a dingy red flag of the same shade as the whiskers of the stroke oar. A coxswain being appointed, and all other matters adjusted, the eight gentlemen threw themselves into strong paroxysms, and pulled up with the tide, stimulated by the compassionate remarks of the ladies, who one and all exclaimed, that it seemed an immense exertion—as indeed it did. At first we raced the other boat, which came alongside in gallant style; but this being found an unpleasant amusement, as giving rise to a great quantity of splashing, and rendering the cold pies and other viands very moist, it was unanimously voted down, and we were suffered to shoot a-head, while the second boat followed ingloriously in our wake.

It was at this time that we first recognised Mr. Leaver. There were two firemen-watermen in the boat, lying by until somebody was exhausted; and one of them, who had taken upon himself the direction of affairs, was heard to cry in a gruff voice, "Pull away, number two—give it her, number two—take a longer reach, number two—now, number two, sir, think you're winning a boat." The greater part of the company had no doubt begun to wonder which of the striped Guernseys it might be that stood in need of such encouragement, when a stifled shriek from Mrs. Leaver confirmed the doubtful and informed the ignorant; and Mr. Leaver, still further disguised in a straw hat and no neckcloth, was observed to be in a fearful perspiration, and failing visibly. Nor was the general consternation diminished at this instant by the same gentleman (in the performance of an accidental aquatic feat, termed "catching a crab") plunging suddenly backward, and displaying nothing of himself to the company, but two violently struggling legs. Mrs. Leaver shrieked again several times, and cried piteously—"Is he dead? Tell me the worst. Is he dead?"

Now, a moment's reflection might have convinced the loving wife, that unless her husband were endowed with some most surprising powers of muscular action, he never could be dead while he kicked so hard; but still Mrs. Leaver cried, "Is he dead? is he dead?" and still everybody else cried—"No, no, no," until such time as Mr. Leaver was replaced in a sitting posture, and his oar (which had been going through all kinds of wrong-headed performances on its own account) was once more put in his hand, by the exertions of the two firemen-watermen. Mrs. Leaver then exclaimed, "Augustus, my child, come to me;" and Mr. Leaver said, "Augusta, my love, compose yourself, I am not injured." But Mrs. Leaver cried again more piteously than before, "Augustus, my child, come to me;" and now the company generally, who seemed to be apprehensive that if Mr. Leaver remained where he was, he might contribute more than his proper share towards the drowning of the party, disinterestedly took part with Mrs. Leaver, and said he really ought to go, and that he was not strong enough for such violent exercise, and ought never to have undertaken it. Reluctantly, Mr. Leaver went, and laid himself down at Mrs. Leaver's feet, and Mrs. Leaver stooping over him, said, "Oh Augustus, how could you terrify me so?" and Mr. Leaver said, "Augusta, my sweet, I never meant to terrify you;" and Mrs. Leaver said, "You are faint, my dear;" and Mr. Leaver said, "I am rather so, my love;" and they were very loving indeed under Mrs. Leaver's veil, until at length Mr. Leaver came forth again, and pleasantly asked if he had not heard something said about bottled stout and sandwiches.

Mrs. Starling, who was one of the party, was perfectly delighted with this scene, and frequently murmured half-aside,

"What a loving couple you are!" or "How delightful it is to see man and wife so happy together!" To us she was quite poetical, (for we are a kind of cousins,) observing that hearts beating in unison like that made life a paradise of sweets; and that when kindred creatures were drawn together by sympathies so fine and delicate, what more than mortal happiness did not our souls partake! To all this we answered "Certainly," or "Very true," or merely sighed, as the case might be. At every new act of the loving couple, the widow's admiration broke out afresh; and when Mrs. Leaver would not permit Mr. Leaver to keep his hat off, lest the sun should strike to his head, and give him a brain fever, Mrs. Starling actually shed tears, and said it reminded her of Adam and Eve.

The loving couple were thus loving all the way to Twickenham, but when we arrived there (by which time the amateur crew looked very thirsty and vicious) they were more playful than ever, for Mrs. Leaver threw stones at Mr. Leaver, and Mr. Leaver ran after Mrs. Leaver on the grass, in a most innocent and enchanting manner. At dinner, too, Mr. Leaver *would* steal Mrs. Leaver's tongue, and Mrs. Leaver *would* retaliate upon Mr. Leaver's fowl; and when Mrs. Leaver was going to take some lobster salad, Mr. Leaver wouldn't let her have any, saying that it made her ill, and she was always sorry for it afterwards, which afforded Mrs. Leaver an opportunity of pretending to be cross, and showing many other prettinesses. But this was merely the smiling surface of their loves, not the mighty depths of the stream, down to which the company, to say the truth, dived rather unexpectedly, from the following accident. It chanced that Mr. Leaver took upon himself to propose the bachelors who had first originated the notion of that entertainment, in doing which, he affected to regret that he was no longer of their body himself, and pretended grievously to lament his fallen state. This Mrs. Leaver's feelings could not brook, even in jest, and consequently, exclaiming aloud, "He loves me not, he loves me not!" she fell in a very pitiable state into the arms of Mrs. Starling, and, directly becoming insensible, was conveyed by that lady and her husband into another room. Presently Mr. Leaver came running back to know if there was a medical gentleman in company, and as there was, (in what company is there not?) both Mr. Leaver and the medical gentleman hurried away together.

The medical gentleman was the first who returned, and among his intimate friends he was observed to laugh and wink, and look as unmedical as might be; but when Mr. Leaver came back he was very solemn, and in answer to all inquiries, shook his head, and remarked that Augusta was far too sensitive to be trifled with—an opinion which the widow subsequently confirmed. Finding that she was in no imminent peril, however, the rest of the party betook themselves to dancing on the green, and very merry and happy they were, and a vast quantity of flirtation there was; the last circumstance being no doubt attributable partly to the fineness of the weather, and partly to the locality, which is well known to be favourable to all harmless recreations.

In the bustle of the scene, Mr. and Mrs. Leaver stole down to the boat, and disposed themselves under the awning, Mrs. Leaver reclining her head upon Mr. Leaver's shoulder, and Mr. Leaver grasping her hand with great fervour, and looking in her face from time to time with a melancholy and sympathetic aspect. The widow sat apart, feigning to be occupied with a book, but stealthily observing them from behind her fan; and the two firemen-watermen, smoking

The Loving Couple

their pipes on the bank hard by, nudged each other, and grinned in enjoyment of the joke. Very few of the party missed the loving couple; and the few who did, heartily congratulated each other on their disappearance.

𝕿HE 𝕮ONTRADICTORY 𝕮OUPLE

—◆—

𝕺NE would suppose that two people who are to pass their whole lives together, and must necessarily be very often alone with each other, could find little pleasure in mutual contradiction; and yet what is more common than a contradictory couple?

The contradictory couple agree in nothing but contradiction. They return home from Mrs. Bluebottle's dinner-party, each in an opposite corner of the coach, and do not exchange a syllable until they have been seated for at least twenty minutes by the fire-side at home, when the gentleman, raising his eyes from the stove, all at once breaks silence:

"What a very extraordinary thing it is," says he, "that you *will* contradict, Charlotte?" "*I* contradict!" cries the lady, "but that's just like you." "What's like me?" says the gentleman sharply. "Saying that I contradict you," replies the lady. "Do you mean to say that you do *not* contradict me?" retorts the gentleman; "do you mean to say that you have not been contradicting me the whole of this day? Do you mean to tell me now, that you have not?" "I mean to tell you nothing of the kind," replies the lady quietly; "when you are wrong, of course I shall contradict you."

During this dialogue the gentleman has been taking his brandy-and-water on one side of the fire, and the lady, with her dressing-case on the table, has been curling her hair on the other. She now lets down her back hair, and proceeds to brush it; preserving at the same time an air of conscious rectitude and suffering virtue, which is intended to exasperate the gentleman, and does so.

"I do believe," he says, taking the spoon out of his glass, and tossing it on the table, "that of all the obstinate, positive, wrong-headed creatures that were ever born, you are the most so, Charlotte." "Certainly, certainly, have it your own way, pray. You see how much *I* contradict you," rejoins the lady. "Of course! you didn't contradict me at dinner-time—oh no, not you!" says the gentleman. "Yes I did," says the lady. "Oh, you did," cries the gentleman; "you admit that?" "If you call that contradiction, I do," the lady answers; "and I say again, Edward, that when I know you are wrong, I will contradict you. I am not your slave." "Not my slave!" repeats the gentleman bitterly; "and you still mean to say that in the Blackburns' new house there are not more than fourteen doors, including the door of the wine-cellar!" "I mean to say," retorts the lady, beating time with her hair-brush on the palm of her hand, "that in that house there are fourteen doors and no more." "Well then—" cries the gentleman, rising in despair, and pacing the room with rapid strides. "By Jove, this is enough to destroy a man's intellect, and drive him mad!"

By and by the gentleman comes to a little, and passing his hand gloomily across his forehead, reseats himself in his former chair. There is a long silence, and this time the lady begins. "I appealed to Mr. Jenkins, who sat next to me on the sofa in the drawing-room during tea—" "Morgan, you mean," interrupts the gentleman. "I do not mean anything of the kind," answers the lady. "Now, by all that is aggravating and impossible to bear," cries the gentleman, clenching his hands and looking upwards in agony, "she is going to insist upon it that Morgan is Jenkins!" "Do you take me for a perfect fool?" exclaims the lady; "do you suppose I don't know the one from the other? Do you suppose I don't know that the man in the blue coat was Mr. Jenkins?" "Jenkins in a blue coat!" cries the gentleman with a groan; "Jenkins in a blue coat! a man who would suffer death rather than wear anything but brown!" "Do you dare to charge me with telling an untruth?" demands the lady, bursting into tears. "I charge you, ma'am," retorts the gentleman, starting up, "with being a monster of contradiction, a monster of aggravation, a—a—a—Jenkins in a blue coat!—what have I done that I should be doomed to hear such statements!"

Expressing himself with great scorn and anguish, the gentleman takes up his candle and stalks off to bed, where feigning to be fast asleep when the lady comes up stairs drowned in tears, murmuring lamentations over her hard fate and indistinct intentions of consulting her brothers, he undergoes the secret torture of hearing her exclaim between whiles, "I know there are only fourteen doors in the house, I know it was Mr. Jenkins, I know he had a blue coat on; and I would say it as positively as I do now, if they were the last words I had to speak!"

If the contradictory couple are blessed with children, they are not the less contradictory on that account. Master James and Miss Charlotte present themselves after dinner, and being in perfect good humour, and finding their parents in the same amiable state, augur from these appearances half a glass of wine a-piece and other extraordinary indulgences. But unfortunately Master James, growing talkative upon such prospects, asks his mamma how tall Mrs. Parsons is, and whether she is not six feet high; to which his mamma replies, "Yes, she should think she was, for Mrs. Parsons is a very tall lady indeed—quite a giantess." "For Heaven's sake, Charlotte," cries her husband, "do not tell the child such preposterous nonsense. Six feet high!" "Well," replies the lady, "surely I may be permitted to have an opinion; my opinion is, that she is six feet high—at least six feet." "Now you know, Charlotte," retorts the gentleman sternly, "that that is *not* your opinion—that you have no such idea—and that you only say this for the sake of contradiction." "You are exceedingly polite," his wife replies; "to be wrong about such a paltry question as anybody's height, would be no great crime; but I say again, that I believe Mrs. Parsons to be six feet—more than six feet; nay, I believe you know her to be full six feet, and only say she is not, because I say she is." This taunt disposes the gentleman to become violent, but he checks himself, and is content to mutter, in a haughty tone, "Six feet—ha! ha! Mrs. Parsons six feet!" and the lady answers, "Yes, six feet. I am sure I am glad you are amused, and I'll say it again—six feet." Thus the subject gradually drops off, and the contradiction begins to be forgotten, when Master James, with some undefined notion of making himself agreeable, and putting things to rights again, unfortunately asks his mamma what the moon's made of; which gives her occasion to say that he had better not ask her, for she is always wrong and never can be right; that he only exposes her to contradiction by asking any question of her; and that he had better ask his papa, who is infallible, and never can be wrong. Papa, smarting under this attack, gives a terrible pull at the bell, and says that if the conversation is to proceed in this way, the children had better be removed. Removed they are, after a few tears and many struggles; and Pa having looked at Ma sideways for a minute or two, with a baleful eye, draws his pocket-handkerchief over his face, and composes himself for his after-dinner nap.

The friends of the contradictory couple often deplore their frequent disputes, though they rather make light of them at the same time: observing, that there is no doubt they are very much attached to each other, and that they never quarrel except about trifles. But neither the friends of the contradictory couple, nor the contradictory couple themselves, reflect, that as the most stupendous objects in nature are but vast collections of minute particles, so the slightest and least considered trifles make up the sum of human happiness or misery.

The Couple Who Dote Upon Their Children

———•———

The couple who dote upon their children have usually a great many of them: six or eight at least. The children are either the healthiest in all the world, or the most unfortunate in existence. In either case, they are equally the theme of their doting parents, and equally a source of mental anguish and irritation to their doting parents' friends.

The couple who dote upon their children recognise no dates but those connected with their births, accidents, illnesses, or remarkable deeds. They keep a mental almanack with a vast number of Innocents' days, all in red letters. They recollect the last coronation, because on that day little Tom fell down the kitchen stairs; the anniversary of the Gunpowder Plot, because it was on the fifth of November that Ned asked whether wooden legs were made in heaven and cocked hats grew in gardens. Mrs. Whiffler will never cease to recollect the last day of the old year as long as she lives, for it was on that day that the baby had the four red spots on its nose which they took for measles: nor Christmas day, for twenty-one days after Christmas day the twins were born; nor Good Friday, for it was on a Good Friday that she was frightened by the donkey-cart when she was in the family way with Georgiana. The moveable feasts have no motion for Mr. and Mrs. Whiffler, but remain pinned down tight and fast to the shoulders of some small child, from whom they can never be separated any more. Time was made, according to their creed, not for slaves, but for girls and boys; the restless sands in his glass are but little children at play.

As we have already intimated, the children of this couple can know no medium. They are either prodigies of good health or prodigies of bad health; whatever they are, they must be prodigies. Mr. Whiffler must have to describe at his office such excruciating agonies constantly undergone by his eldest boy, as nobody else's eldest boy ever underwent; or he must be able to declare that there never was a child endowed with such amazing health, such an indomitable constitution, and such a cast-iron frame, as his child. His children must be, in some respect or other, above and beyond the children of all other people. To such an extent is this feeling pushed, that we were once slightly acquainted with a lady and gentleman who carried their heads so high and became so proud after their youngest child fell out of a two-pair-of-stairs window without hurting himself much, that the greater part of their friends were obliged to forego their acquaintance. But perhaps this may be an extreme case, and one not justly entitled to be considered as a precedent of general application.

If a friend happen to dine in a friendly way with one of these couples who dote upon their children, it is nearly impossible for him to divert the conversation from their favourite topic. Everything reminds Mr. Whiffler of Ned, or Mrs. Whiffler of Mary Anne, or of the time before Ned was born, or the time before Mary Anne was thought of. The slightest remark, however harmless in itself, will awaken slumbering recollections of the twins. It is impossible to steer clear of them. They will come uppermost, let the poor man do what he may. Ned has been known to be lost sight of for half an hour, Dick has been forgotten, the name of Mary Anne has not been mentioned, but the twins will out. Nothing can keep down the twins.

"It's a very extraordinary thing, Saunders," says Mr. Whiffler to the visitor—"but—you have seen our little babies, the—the—twins?" The friend's heart sinks within him as he answers, "Oh, yes—often." "Your talking of the Pyramids," says Mr. Whiffler, quite as a matter of course, "reminds me of the twins. It's a very extraordinary thing about those babies—what colour should you say their eyes were?" "Upon my word," the friend stammers, "I hardly know how to answer"—the fact being, that except as the friend does not remember to have heard of any departure from the ordinary course of nature in the instance of these twins, they might have no eyes at all for aught he has observed to the contrary. "You wouldn't say they

The Couple who Dote upon their Children

were red, I suppose?" says Mr. Whiffler. The friend hesitates, and rather thinks they are; but inferring from the expression of Mr. Whiffler's face that red is not the colour, smiles with some confidence, and says, "No, no! very different from that." "What should you say to blue?" says Mr. Whiffler. The friend glances at him, and observing a different expression in his face, ventures to say, "I should say they *were* blue—a decided blue." "To be sure!" cries Mr. Whiffler, triumphantly. "I knew you would! But what should you say if I was to tell you that the boy's eyes are blue and the girl's hazel, eh?" "Impossible!" exclaims the friend, not at all knowing why it should be impossible. "A fact, notwithstanding," cries Mr. Whiffler; "and let me tell you, Saunders, *that's* not a common thing in twins, or a circumstance that'll happen every day."

In this dialogue Mrs. Whiffler, as being deeply responsible for the twins, their charms and singularities, has taken no share; but she now relates, in broken English, a witticism of little Dick's bearing upon the subject just discussed, which delights Mr. Whiffler beyond measure, and causes him to declare that he would have sworn that was Dick's if he had heard it anywhere. Then he requests that Mrs. Whiffler will tell Saunders what Tom said about mad bulls; and Mrs. Whiffler relating the anecdote, a discussion ensues upon the different character of Tom's wit and Dick's wit, from which it appears that Dick's humour is of a lively turn, while Tom's style is dry and caustic. This discussion being enlivened by various illustrations, lasts a long time, and is only stopped by Mrs. Whiffler instructing the footman to ring the nursery bell, as the children were promised that they should come down and taste the pudding.

The friend turns pale when this order is given, and paler still when it is followed up by a great pattering on the staircase, (not unlike the sound of rain upon a skylight,) a violent bursting open of the dining-room door, and the tumultuous appearance of six small children, closely succeeded by a strong nursery-maid with a twin in each arm. As the whole eight are screaming, shouting, or kicking—some influenced by a ravenous appetite, some by a horror of the stranger, and some by a conflict of the two feelings—a pretty long space elapses before all their heads can be ranged round the table and anything like order restored; in bringing about which happy state of things both the nurse and footman are severely scratched. At length Mrs. Whiffler is heard to say, "Mr. Saunders, shall I give you some pudding?" A breathless silence ensues, and sixteen small eyes are fixed upon the guest in expectation of his reply. A wild shout of joy proclaims that he has said "No, thank you." Spoons are waved in the air, legs appear above the table-cloth in uncontrollable ecstasy and eighty short fingers dabble in damson syrup.

While the pudding is being disposed of, Mr. and Mrs. Whiffler look on with beaming countenances, and Mr. Whiffler nudging his friend Saunders, begs him to take notice of Tom's eyes, or Dick's chin, or Ned's nose, or Mary Anne's hair, or Emily's figure, or little Bob's calves, or Fanny's mouth, or Cary's head, as the case may be. Whatever the attention of Mr. Saunders is called to, Mr. Saunders admires of course; though he is rather confused about the sex of the youngest branches and looks at the wrong children, turning to a girl when Mr. Whiffler directs his attention to a boy, and falling into raptures with a boy when he ought to be enchanted with a girl. Then the dessert comes, and there is a vast deal of scrambling after fruit, and sudden spirting forth of juice out of tight oranges into infant eyes, and much screeching and wailing in consequence. At length it becomes time for Mrs. Whiffler to retire, and all the children are by force of arms compelled to kiss and love Mr. Saunders before going up-stairs, except Tom, who, lying on his back in the hall, proclaims that Mr. Saunders "is a naughty beast;" and Dick, who having drunk his father's wine when he was looking another way, is found to be intoxicated and is carried out, very limp and helpless.

Mr. Whiffler and his friend are left alone together, but Mr. Whiffler's thoughts are still with his family, if his family are not with him. "Saunders," says he, after a short silence, "if you please, we'll drink Mrs. Whiffler and the children." Mr. Saunders feels this to be a reproach against himself for not proposing the same sentiment, and drinks it in some confusion. "Ah!" Mr. Whiffler sighs, "these children, Saunders, make one quite an old man." Mr. Saunders thinks that if they were his, they would make him a very old man; but he says nothing. "And yet," pursues Mr. Whiffler, "what can equal domestic happiness? what can equal the engaging ways of children! Saunders, why don't *you* get married?" Now, this is an embarrassing question, because Mr. Saunders has been thinking that if he had at any time entertained matrimonial designs, the revelation of that day would surely have routed them for ever. "I am glad, however," says Mr. Whiffler, "that you *are* a bachelor,—glad on one account, Saunders; a selfish one, I admit. Will you do Mrs. Whiffler and myself a favour?" Mr. Saunders is surprised—evidently surprised; but he replies, "With the greatest pleasure." "Then, will you, Saunders," says Mr. Whiffler, in an impressive manner, "will you cement and consolidate our friendship by coming into the family (so to speak) as a godfather?" "I shall be proud and delighted," replies Mr. Saunders: "which of the children is it?

Really, I thought they were all christened; or—" "Saunders," Mr. Whiffler interposes, "they *are* all christened; you are right. The fact is, that Mrs. Whiffler is—in short, we expect another." "Not a ninth?" cries the friend, all aghast at the idea. "Yes, Saunders," rejoins Mr. Whiffler, solemnly, "a ninth. Did we drink Mrs. Whiffler's health? Let us drink it again, Saunders, and wish her well over it!"

Doctor Johnson used to tell a story of a man who had but one idea, which was a wrong one. The couple who dote upon their children are in the same predicament: at home or abroad, at all times, and in all places, their thoughts are bound up in this one subject, and have no sphere beyond. They relate the clever things their offspring say or do, and weary every company with their prolixity and absurdity. Mr. Whiffler takes a friend by the button at a street corner on a windy day to tell him a *bon mot* of his youngest boy's; and Mrs. Whiffler, calling to see a sick acquaintance, entertains her with a cheerful account of all her own past sufferings and present expectations. In such cases the sins of the fathers indeed descend upon the children; for people soon come to regard them as predestined little bores. The couple who dote upon their children cannot be said to be actuated by a general love for these engaging little people (which would be a great excuse); for they are apt to underrate and entertain a jealousy of any children but their own. If they examined their own hearts, they would, perhaps, find at the bottom of all this more self-love and egotism than they think of. Self-love and egotism are bad qualities, of which the unrestrained exhibition, though it may be sometimes amusing, never fails to be wearisome and unpleasant. Couples who dote upon their children, therefore, are best avoided.

THE COOL COUPLE

———

THERE is an old fashioned weather-glass representing a house with two doorways, in one of which is the figure of a gentleman, in the other the figure of a lady. When the weather is to be fine the lady comes out and the gentleman goes in; when wet, the gentleman comes out and the lady goes in. They never seek each other's society, are never elevated and depressed by the same cause, and have nothing in common. They are the model of a cool couple, except that there is something of politeness and consideration about the behaviour of the gentleman in the weather-glass, in which, neither of the cool couple can be said to participate.

The cool couple are seldom alone together, and when they are, nothing can exceed their apathy and dulness: the gentleman being for the most part drowsy, and the lady silent. If they enter into conversation, it is usually of an ironical or recriminatory nature. Thus, when the gentleman has indulged in a very long yawn and settled himself more snugly into his easy-chair, the lady will perhaps remark, "Well, I am sure, Charles! I hope you're comfortable." To which the gentleman replies, "Oh yes, he's quite comfortable—quite." "There are not many married men, I hope," returns the lady, "who seek comfort in such selfish gratifications as you do." "Nor many wives who seek comfort in such selfish gratifications as *you* do, I hope," retorts the gentleman. "Whose fault is that?" demands the lady. The gentleman becoming more sleepy, returns no answer. "Whose fault is that?" the lady repeats.

The gentleman still returning no answer, she goes on to say that she believes there never was in all this world anybody so attached to her home, so thoroughly domestic, so unwilling to seek a moment's gratification or pleasure beyond her own fireside as she. God knows that before she was married she never thought or dreamt of such a thing; and she remembers that her poor papa used to say again and again, almost every day of his life, "Oh, my dear Louisa, if you only marry a man who understands you, and takes the trouble to consider your happiness and accommodate himself a very little to your disposition, what a treasure he will find in you!" She supposes her papa knew what her disposition was—he had known her long enough—he ought to have been acquainted with it; but what can she do? If her home is always dull and lonely, and her husband is always absent and finds no pleasure in her society, she is naturally sometimes driven (seldom enough, she is sure) to seek a little recreation elsewhere; she is not expected to pine and mope to death, she hopes. "Then come, Louisa," says the gentleman, waking up as suddenly as he fell asleep, "stop at home this evening, and so will I." "I should be sorry to suppose, Charles, that you took a pleasure in aggravating me," replies the lady; "but you know as well as I do that I am particularly engaged to Mrs. Mortimer, and that it would be an act of the grossest rudeness and ill-breeding, after accepting a seat in her box and preventing her from inviting anybody else, not to go." "Ah! there it is!" says the gentleman, shrugging his shoulders, "I knew that perfectly well. I knew you couldn't devote an evening to your own home. Now all I have to say, Louisa, is this—recollect that *I* was quite willing to stay at home, and that it's no fault of *mine* we are not oftener together."

The Cool Couple

With that the gentleman goes away to keep an old appointment at his club, and the lady hurries off to dress for Mrs. Mortimer's; and neither thinks of the other until by some odd chance they find themselves alone again.

But it must not be supposed that the cool couple are habitually a quarrelsome one. Quite the contrary. These differences are only occasions for a little self-excuse,—nothing more. In general they are as easy and careless, and dispute as seldom, as any common acquaintances may; for it is neither worth their while to put each other out of the way, nor to ruffle themselves.

When they meet in society, the cool couple are the best-bred people in existence. The lady is seated in a corner among a little knot of lady friends, one of whom exclaims, "why, I vow and declare there is your husband, my dear!" "Whose?—mine?" she says carelessly. "Ay, yours, and coming this way too." "How very odd!" says the lady, in a languid tone, "I thought he had been at Dover." The gentleman coming up, and speaking to all the other ladies and nodding slightly to his wife, it turns out that he has been at Dover, and has just now returned. "What a strange creature you are!" cries his wife; "and what on earth brought you here, I wonder?" "I came to look after you, *of course*," rejoins her husband. This is so pleasant a jest that the lady is mightily amused, as are all the other ladies similarly situated who are within hearing; and while they are enjoying it to the full, the gentleman nods again, turns upon his heel, and saunters away.

There are times, however, when his company is not so agreeable, though equally unexpected; such as when the lady has invited one or two particular friends to tea and scandal, and he happens to come home in the very midst of their diversion. It is a hundred chances to one that he does not remain in the house half an hour, but the lady is rather disturbed by the intrusion, notwithstanding, and reasons within herself: "I am sure I never interfere with him, and why should he interfere with me? It can scarcely be accidental; it never happens that I have a particular reason for not wishing him to come home, but he always comes. It's very provoking and tiresome; and I am sure when he leaves me so much alone for his own pleasure, the least he could do would be to do as much for mine." Observing what passes in her mind, the gentleman, who has come home for his own accommodation, makes a merit of it with himself; arrives at the conclusion that it is the very last place in which he can hope to be comfortable; and determines, as he takes up his hat and cane, never to be so virtuous again.

Thus a great many cool couples go on until they are cold couples, and the grave has closed over their folly and indifference. Loss of name, station, character, life itself, has ensued from causes as slight as these, before now; and when gossips tell such tales, and aggravate their deformities, they elevate their hands and eyebrows, and call each other to witness what a cool couple Mr. and Mrs. So-and-So always were, even in the best of times.

THE PLAUSIBLE COUPLE

THE plausible couple have many titles. They are "a delightful couple," "an affectionate couple," "a most agreeable couple," "a good-hearted couple," and "the best-natured couple in existence." The truth is, that the plausible couple are people of the world; and either the way of pleasing the world has grown much easier than it was in the days of the old man and his ass, or the old man was but a bad hand at it, and knew very little of the trade.

"But is it really possible to please the world?" says some doubting reader. It is indeed. Nay, it is not only very possible, but very easy. The ways are crooked, and sometimes foul and low. What then? A man need but crawl upon his hands and knees, know when to close his eyes and when his ears, when to stoop and when to stand upright; and if by the world is meant that atom of it in which he moves himself, he shall please it, never fear.

Now, it will be readily seen, that if a plausible man or woman have an easy means of pleasing the world by an adaption of self to all its twistings and twinings, a plausible man *and* woman, or, in other words, a plausible couple, playing into each other's hands, and acting in concert, have a manifest advantage. Hence it is that plausible couples scarcely ever fail of success on a pretty large scale; and hence it is that if the reader, laying down this unwieldy volume at the next full stop, will have the goodness to review his or her circle or acquaintance, and to search particularly for some man and wife with a large connexion and a good name, not easily referable to their abilities or their wealth, he or she (that is, the male or female reader) will certainly find that gentleman or lady, on a very short reflection, to be a plausible couple.

The plausible couple are the most ecstatic people living: the most sensitive people—to merit—on the face of the earth. Nothing clever or virtuous escapes them. They have microscopic eyes for such endowments, and can find them anywhere. The plausible couple never fawn—oh no! They don't even scruple to tell their friends of their faults. One is too generous, another too candid; a third has a tendency to think all people like himself, and to regard mankind as a company of angels; a fourth is kind-hearted to a fault. "We never flatter, my dear Mrs. Jackson," say the plausible couple; "we speak our minds. Neither you nor Mr. Jackson have faults enough. It may sound strangely, but it is true. You have not faults enough. You know our way,—we must speak out, and always do. Quarrel with us for saying so, if you will; but we repeat it,—you have not faults enough!"

The plausible couple are no less plausible to each other than to third parties. They are always loving and harmonious. The plausible gentleman calls his wife "darling," and the plausible lady addresses him as "dearest." If it be Mr. and Mrs. Bobtail Widger, Mrs. Widger is "Lavinia, darling," and Mr. Widger is "Bobtail, dearest." Speaking of each other, they observe the same tender form. Mrs. Widger relates what "Bobtail" said, and Mr. Widger recounts what "darling" thought and did.

If you sit next to the plausible lady at a dinner-table, she takes the earliest opportunity of expressing her belief that you are acquainted with the Clickits; she is sure she has heard the Clickits speak of you—she must not tell you in what terms, or you will take her for a flatterer. You admit a knowledge of the Clickits; the plausible lady immediately launches out in their praise. She quite loves the Clickits. Were there ever such true-hearted, hospitable, excellent people—such a gentle, interesting little woman as Mrs. Clickit, or such a frank, unaffected creature as Mr. Clickit? were there ever two people, in short, so little spoiled by the world as they are? "As who, darling?" cries

The Plausible Couple

Mr. Widger, from the opposite side of the table. "The Clickits, dearest," replies Mrs. Widger. "Indeed you are right, darling," Mr. Widger rejoins; "the Clickits are a very high-minded, worthy, estimable couple." Mrs. Widger remarking that Bobtail always grows quite eloquent upon this subject, Mr. Widger admits that he feels very strongly whenever such people as the Clickits and some other friends of his (here he glances at the host and hostess) are mentioned; for they are an honour to human nature, and do one good to think of. "*You* know the Clickits, Mrs. Jackson?" he says, addressing the lady of the house. "No, indeed; we have not that pleasure," she replies. "You astonish me!" exclaims Mr. Widger: "not know the Clickits! why, you are the very people of all others who ought to be their bosom friends. You are kindred beings; you are one and the same thing:—not know the Clickits! Now *will* you know the Clickits? Will you make a point of knowing them? Will you meet them in a friendly way at our house one evening, and be acquainted with them?" Mrs. Jackson will be quite delighted; nothing would give her more pleasure. "Then, Lavinia, my darling," says Mr. Widger, "mind you don't lose sight of that; now, pray take care that Mr. and Mrs. Jackson know the Clickits without loss of time. Such people ought not to be strangers to each other." Mrs. Widger books both families as the centre of attraction for her next party; and Mr. Widger, going on to expatiate upon the virtues of the Clickits, adds to their other moral qualities, that they keep one of the neatest phaetons in town, and have two thousand a year.

As the plausible couple never laud the merits of any absent person, without dexterously contriving that their praises shall reflect upon somebody who is present, so they never depreciate anything or anybody, without turning their depreciation to the same account. Their friend, Mr. Slummery, say they, is unquestionably a clever painter, and would no doubt be very popular, and sell his pictures at a very high price, if that cruel Mr. Fithers had not forestalled him in his department of art, and made it thoroughly and completely his own;—Fithers, it is to be observed, being present and within hearing, and Slummery elsewhere. Is Mrs. Tabblewick really as beautiful as people say? Why, there indeed you ask them a very puzzling question, because there is no doubt that she is a very charming woman, and they have long known her intimately. She is no doubt beautiful, very beautiful; they once thought her the most beautiful woman ever seen; still if you press them for an honest answer, they are bound to say that this was before they had ever seen our lovely friend on the sofa (the sofa is hard by, and our lovely friend can't help hearing the whispers in which this is said); since that time, perhaps, they have been hardly fair judges; Mrs. Tabblewick is no doubt extremely handsome,—very like our friend, in fact, in the form of the features,—but in point of expression, and soul, and figure, and air altogether—oh dear!

But while the plausible couple depreciate, they are still careful to preserve their character for amiability and kind feeling; indeed the depreciation itself is often made to grow out of their excessive sympathy and good-will. The plausible lady calls on a lady who dotes upon her children, and is sitting with a little girl upon her knee, enraptured by her artless replies, and protesting that there is nothing she delights in so much as conversing with these fairies; when the other lady inquires if she has seen young Mrs. Finching lately, and whether the baby has turned out a finer one than it promised to be. "Oh dear!" cries the plausible lady, "you cannot think how often Bobtail and I have talked about poor Mrs. Finching—she is such a dear soul, and was so anxious that the baby should be a fine child—and very naturally, because she was very much here at one time, and there is, you know, a natural emulation among mothers—that it is impossible to tell you how much we have felt for her." "Is it weak or plain, or what?" inquires the other. "Weak or plain, my love," returns the plausible lady, "it's a fright—a perfect little fright; you never saw such a miserable creature in all your days. Positively you must not let her see one of these beautiful dears again, or you'll break her heart, you will indeed.—Heaven bless this child, see how she is looking in my face! can you conceive anything prettier than that? If poor Mrs. Finching could only hope—but that's impossible—and the gifts of Providence, you know—What *did* I do with my pocket handkerchief!"

What prompts the mother, who dotes upon her children, to comment to her lord that evening on the plausible lady's engaging qualities and feeling heart? and what is it that procures Mr. and Mrs. Bobtail Widger an immediate invitation to dinner?

⚑he ℕice 𝔏ittle ℭouple

———◆———

A CUSTOM once prevailed in old-fashioned circles, that when a lady or gentleman was unable to sing a song, he or she should enliven the company with a story. As we find ourself in the predicament of not being able to describe (to our own satisfaction) nice little couples in the abstract, we purpose telling in this place a little story about a nice little couple of our acquaintance.

Mr. and Mrs. Chirrup are the nice little couple in question. Mr. Chirrup has the smartness, and something of the brisk, quick manner of a small bird. Mrs. Chirrup is the prettiest of all little women, and has the prettiest little figure conceivable. She has the neatest little foot, and the softest little voice, and the pleasantest little smile, and the tidiest little curls, and the brightest little eyes, and the quietest little manner, and is, in short, altogether one of the most engaging of all little women, dead or alive. She is a condensation of all the domestic virtues,—a pocket edition of the Young Man's Best Companion,—a little woman at a very high pressure, with an amazing quantity of goodness and usefulness in an exceedingly small space. Little as she is, Mrs. Chirrup might furnish forth matter for the moral equipment of a score of housewives, six feet high in their stockings—if, in the presence of ladies, we may be allowed the expression—and of corresponding robustness.

Nobody knows all this better than Mr. Chirrup, though he rather takes on that he don't. Accordingly he is very proud of his better-half, and evidently considers himself, as all other people consider him, rather fortunate in having her to wife. We say evidently, because Mr. Chirrup is a warm-hearted little fellow; and if you catch his eye when he has been slily glancing at Mrs. Chirrup in company, there is a certain complacent twinkle in it, accompanied, perhaps, by a half-expressed toss of the head, which as clearly indicates what has been passing in his mind as if he had put it into words, and shouted it out through a speaking-trumpet. Moreover,

The Nice Little Couple

Mr. Chirrup has a particularly mild and bird-like manner of calling Mrs. Chirrup "my dear;" and—for he is of a jocose turn—of cutting little witticisms upon her, and making her the subject of various harmless pleasantries, which nobody enjoys more thoroughly than Mrs. Chirrup herself. Mr. Chirrup, too, now and then affects to deplore his bachelor-days, and to bemoan (with a marvellously contented and smirking face) the loss of his freedom, and the sorrow of his heart at having been taken captive by Mrs. Chirrup—all of which circumstances combine to show the secret triumph and satisfaction of Mr. Chirrup's soul.

We have already had occasion to observe that Mrs. Chirrup is an incomparable housewife. In all the arts of domestic arrangement and management, in all the mysteries of confectionary-making, pickling, and preserving, never was such a thorough adept as that nice little body. She is, besides, a cunning worker in muslin and fine linen, and a special hand at marketing to the very best advantage. But if there be one branch of housekeeping in which she excels to an utterly unparalleled and unprecedented extent, it is in the important one of carving. A roast goose is universally allowed to be the great stumbling-block in the way of young aspirants to perfection in this department of science; many promising carvers, beginning with legs of mutton, and preserving a good reputation through fillets of veal, sirloins of beef, quarters of lamb, fowls, and even ducks, have sunk before a roast goose, and lost caste and character for ever. To Mrs. Chirrup the resolving a goose into its smallest component parts is a pleasant pastime—a practical joke—a thing to be done in a minute or so, without the smallest interruption to the conversation of the time. No handing the dish over to an unfortunate man upon her right or left, no wild sharpening of the knife, no hacking and sawing at an unruly joint, no noise, no splash, no heat, no leaving off in despair; all is confidence and cheerfulness. The dish is set upon the table, the cover is removed; for an instant, and only an instant, you observe that Mrs. Chirrup's attention is distracted; she smiles, but heareth not. You proceed with your story; meanwhile the glittering knife is slowly upraised, both Mrs. Chirrup's wrists are slightly but not ungracefully agitated, she compresses her lips for an instant, then breaks into a smile, and all is over. The legs of the bird slide gently down into a pool of gravy, the wings seem to melt from the body, the breast separates into a row of juicy slices, the smaller and more complicated parts of his anatomy are perfectly developed, a cavern of stuffing is revealed, and the goose is gone!

To dine with Mr. and Mrs. Chirrup is one of the pleasantest things in the world. Mr. Chirrup has a bachelor friend, who lived with him in his own days of single blessedness, and to whom he is mightily attached. Contrary to the usual custom, this bachelor friend is no less a friend of Mrs. Chirrup's, and, consequently, whenever you dine with Mr. and Mrs. Chirrup, you meet the bachelor friend. It would put any reasonably-conditioned mortal into good humour to observe the entire unanimity which subsists between these three; but there is a quiet welcome dimpling in Mrs. Chirrup's face, a bustling hospitality oozing as it were out of the waistcoat-pockets of Mr. Chirrup, and a patronising enjoyment of their cordiality and satisfaction on the part of the bachelor friend, which is quite delightful. On these occasions Mr. Chirrup usually takes an opportunity of rallying the friend on being single, and the friend retorts upon Mr. Chirrup for being married, at which

The Nice Little Couple

moments some single young ladies present are like to die of laughter; and we have more than once observed them bestow looks upon the friend, which convinces us that his position is by no means a safe one, as, indeed, we hold no bachelor's to be who visits friends and cracks jokes on wedlock, for certain it is that such men walk among traps and nets and pitfalls innumerable, and often find themselves down upon their knees at the altar rails, taking M. or N. for their wedded wives before they know anything about the matter.

However, this is no business of Mr. Chirrup's, who talks, and laughs, and drinks his wine, and laughs again, and talks more, until it is time to repair to the drawing-room, where, coffee served and over, Mrs. Chirrup prepares for a round game, by sorting the nicest possible little fish into the nicest possible little pools, and calling Mr. Chirrup to assist her, which Mr. Chirrup does. As they stand side by side, you find that Mr. Chirrup is the least possible shadow of a shade taller than Mrs. Chirrup, and that they are the neatest and best-matched little couple that can be, which the chances are ten to one against your observing with such effect at any other time, unless you see them in the street arm-in-arm, or meet them some rainy day trotting along under a very small umbrella. The round game (at which Mr. Chirrup is the merriest of the party) being done and over, in course of time a nice little tray appears, on which is a nice little supper; and when that is finished likewise, and you have said "Good night," you find yourself repeating a dozen times, as you ride home, that there never was such a nice little couple as Mr. and Mrs. Chirrup.

Whether it is that pleasant qualities, being packed more closely in small bodies than in large, come more readily to hand than when they are diffused over a wider space, and have to be gathered together for use, we don't know, but as a general rule,—strengthened like all other rules by its exception,—we hold that little people are sprightly and good-natured. The more sprightly and good-natured people we have, the better; therefore, let us wish well to all nice little couples, and hope that they may increase and multiply.

ᛏHE ᛖGOTISTICAL ᛒOUPLE

———◆———

ᛖGOTISM in couples is of two kinds.—It is our purpose to show this by two examples.

The egotistical couple may be young, old, middle-aged, well-to-do, or ill-to-do; they may have a small family, a large family, or no family at all. There is no outward sign by which an egotistical couple may be known and avoided. They come upon you unawares; there is no guarding against them. No man can of himself be forewarned or forearmed against an egotistical couple.

The egotistical couple have undergone every calamity, and experienced every pleasurable and painful sensation of which our nature is susceptible. You cannot by possibility tell the egotistical couple anything they don't know, or describe to them anything they have not felt. They have been everything but dead. Sometimes we are tempted to wish they had been even that, but only in our uncharitable moments, which are few and far between.

We happened the other day, in the course of a morning call, to encounter an egotistical couple, nor were we suffered to remain long in ignorance of the fact, for our very first inquiry of the lady of the house brought them into active and vigorous operation. The inquiry was of course touching the lady's health, and the answer happened to be that she had not been very well. "Oh my dear!" said the egotistical lady, "don't talk of not being well. We have been in *such* a state since we saw you last!" The lady of the house happening to remark that her lord had not been well either, the egotistical gentleman struck in: "Never let Briggs complain of not being well—never let Briggs complain, my dear Mrs. Briggs, after what I have undergone within these six weeks. He doesn't know what it is to be ill, he hasn't the least idea of it; not the faintest conception." "My dear," interposed his wife smiling, "you talk as if it were almost a crime in Mr. Briggs not to have been as ill as we have been, instead of feeling thankful to Providence that both he and our dear Mrs. Briggs are in such blissful ignorance of real suffering." "My love," returned the egotistical gentleman, in a low and pious voice, "you mistake me. I feel grateful—very grateful. I trust our friends may never purchase their experience as dearly as we have bought ours; I hope they never may!"

Having put down Mrs. Briggs upon this theme, and settled the question thus, the egotistical gentleman turned to us, and, after a few preliminary remarks, all tending towards and leading up to the point he had in his mind, inquired if we happened to be acquainted with the Dowager Lady Snorflerer. On our replying in the negative, he presumed we had often met Lord Slang, or beyond all doubt, that we were on intimate terms with Sir Chipkins Glogwog. Finding that we were equally unable to lay claim to either of these distinctions, he expressed great astonishment, and turning to his wife with a retrospective smile, inquired who it was that had told that capital story about the mashed potatoes. "Who, my dear?" returned the egotistical lady, "why Sir Chipkins, of course; how can you ask! Don't you remember his applying it to our cook, and saying that you and I were so like the Prince and Princess that he could almost have sworn we were they?" "To be sure, I remember that," said the egotistical gentleman, "but are you quite certain that didn't apply to the other anecdote about the Emperor of Austria and the pump?" "Upon my word then, I think it did," replied his wife. "To be sure it did," said the egotistical gentleman. "It was Slang's story, I remember now, perfectly." However, it turned out, a few seconds afterwards, that the egotistical gentleman's memory was rather treacherous, as he began to have a misgiving that the story had been told by the Dowager Lady Snorflerer the very last time they dined there; but there appearing, on further consideration, strong circumstantial evidence tending to show that this couldn't be, inasmuch as the Dowager Lady Snorflerer had been, on the occasion in question, wholly engrossed by the egotistical lady, the egotistical gentleman recanted this opinion; and after laying the story at the doors of a great many great people, happily left it at last with the Duke of Scuttlewig,—observing that it was not extraordinary he had forgotten his Grace hitherto, as it often happened that the names of those with whom we were upon the most familiar footing were the very last to present themselves to our thoughts.

It not only appeared that the egotistical couple knew everybody, but that scarcely any event of importance or notoriety had occurred for many years with which they had not been in some way or other connected. Thus we learned that when the well-known attempt upon the life of George the Third was made by Hatfield in Drury Lane theatre, the egotistical gentleman's grandfather sat upon his right hand and was the first man who collared him; and that the egotistical lady's aunt, sitting within a few boxes of the royal party, was the only person in the audience who heard his Majesty exclaim, "Charlotte, Charlotte, don't be frightened, don't be frightened—they're letting off squibs—they're letting off squibs." When the fire broke out which ended in the destruction of the two Houses of Parliament, the egotistical couple, being at the time at a drawing-room window on Blackheath, then and there simultaneously exclaimed, to the astonishment of a whole party—"It's the House of Lords!" Nor was this a solitary instance of their peculiar discernment, for chancing to be (as by a comparison of dates and circumstances they afterwards found) in the same omnibus with Mr. Greenacre, when he carried his victim's head about town in a blue bag, they both remarked a singular twitching in the muscles of his countenance; and walking down Fish Street Hill, a few weeks since, the egotistical gentleman said to his lady—slightly casting up his eyes to the top of the Monument—"There's a boy up there, my dear, reading a Bible. It's very strange. I don't like it.—In five seconds afterwards, Sir," says the egotistical gentleman, bringing his hands together with one violent clap—"the lad was over!"

Diversifying these topics by the introduction of many others of the same kind, and entertaining us between whiles with a minute account of what weather and diet agreed with them, and what weather and diet disagreed with them, and at what time they usually got up, and at what time went to bed, with many other particulars of their domestic economy too numerous to mention, the egotistical couple at length took their leave, and afforded us an opportunity of doing the same.

Mr. and Mrs. Sliverstone are an egotistical couple of another class, for all the lady's egotism is about her husband, and all the gentleman's about his wife. For example:—Mr. Sliverstone is a clerical gentleman, and occasionally writes sermons, as clerical gentlemen do. If you happen to obtain admission at the street door while he is so engaged, Mrs. Sliverstone appears on tip-toe, and speaking in a solemn whisper, as if there were at least three or four particular friends up stairs, all upon the point of death, implores you to be very silent, for Mr. Sliverstone is composing, and she need not say how very important it is that he should not be disturbed. Unwilling to interrupt anything so serious, you hasten to withdraw, with many apologies; but this Mrs. Sliverstone will by no means allow, observing, that she knows you would like to see him, as it is very natural you should, and that she is determined to make a trial for you, as you are a great favourite. So you are led up stairs—still on tip-toe—to the door of a little back room, in which, as the lady informs you in a whisper, Mr. Sliverstone always writes. No answer being returned to a couple of soft taps, the lady opens the door, and there, sure enough, is Mr. Sliverstone, with dishevelled hair, powdering away with pen, ink and paper, at a rate which, if he has any power of sustaining it, would settle the longest sermon in no time. At first he is too much absorbed to be roused by this intrusion; but presently looking up, says faintly, "Ah!" and pointing to his desk with a weary and languid smile, extends his hand, and hopes you'll forgive him. Then Mrs. Sliverstone sits down beside him, and taking his hand in hers, tells you how that

Mr. Sliverstone has been shut up there ever since nine o'clock in the morning (it is by this time twelve at noon) and how she knows it cannot be good for his health, and is very uneasy about it. Unto this Mr. Sliverstone replies firmly, that "It must be done;" which agonizes Mrs. Sliverstone still more; and she goes on to tell you that such were Mr. Sliverstone's labours last week—what with the buryings, marryings, churchings, christenings, and all together—that when he was going up the pulpit stairs on Sunday evening, he was obliged to hold on by the rails, or he would certainly have fallen over into his own pew. Mr. Sliverstone, who has been listening and smiling meekly, says, "Not quite so bad as that, not quite so bad!" he admits though, on cross-examination, that he *was* very near falling upon the verger who was following him up to bolt the door; but adds, that it was his duty as a Christian to fall upon him, if need were, and that he, Mr. Sliverstone, and (possibly the verger too) ought to glory in it.

This sentiment communicates new impulse to Mrs. Sliverstone, who launches into new praises of Mr. Sliverstone's worth and excellence, to which he listens in the same meek silence, save when he puts in a word of self-denial relative to some question of face, as—"Not seventy-two christenings that week, my dear. Only seventy-one, only seventy-one." At length his lady has quite concluded, and then he says, Why should he repine, why should he give way, why should he suffer his heart to sink within him? Is it he alone who toils and suffers? What has she gone through, he should like to know? What does she go through every day for him and for society?

With such an exordium Mr. Sliverstone launches out into glowing praises of the conduct of Mrs. Sliverstone in the production of eight young children, and the subsequent rearing and fostering of the same; and thus the husband magnifies the wife, and the wife the husband.

This would be well enough if Mr. and Mrs. Sliverstone kept it to themselves, or even to themselves and a friend or two; but they do not. The more hearers they have, the more egotistical the couple become, and the more anxious they are to make believers in their merits. Perhaps this is the worst kind of egotism. It has not even the poor excuse of being spontaneous, but is the result of a deliberate system and malice aforethought. Mere empty-headed conceit excites our pity, but ostentatious hypocrisy awakens our disgust.

The Couple Who Coddle Themselves

——◆——

Mrs. Merrywinkle's maiden name was Chopper. She was the only child of Mr. and Mrs. Chopper. Her father died when she was, as the play-books express it, "yet an infant;" and so old Mrs. Chopper, when her daughter married, made the house of her son-in-law her home from that time henceforth, and set up her staff of rest with Mr. and Mrs. Merrywinkle.

Mr. and Mrs. Merrywinkle are a couple who coddle themselves; and the venerable Mrs. Chopper is an aider and abettor in the same.

Mr. Merrywinkle is a rather lean and long-necked gentleman, middle-aged and middle-sized, and usually troubled with a cold in the head. Mrs. Merrywinkle is a delicate-looking lady, with very light hair, and is exceedingly subject to the same unpleasant disorder. The venerable Mrs. Chopper—who is strictly entitled to the appellation, her daughter not being very young, otherwise than by courtesy, at the time of her marriage, which was some years ago—is a mysterious old lady who lurks behind a pair of spectacles, and is afflicted with a chronic disease, respecting which she has taken a vast deal of medical advice, and referred to a vast number of medical books, without meeting any definition of symptoms that at all suits her, or enables her to say, "That's my complaint." Indeed, the absence of authentic information upon the subject of this complaint would seem to be Mrs. Chopper's greatest ill, as in all other respects she is an uncommonly hale and hearty woman.

Both Mr. and Mrs. Merrywinkle wear an extraordinary quantity of flannel, and have a habit of putting their feet in hot water to an unnatural extent. They likewise indulge in chamomile tea and such-like compounds, and rub themselves on the slightest provocation with camphorated spirits and other lotions applicable to mumps, sore-throat, rheumatism, or lumbago.

Mr. Merrywinkle's leaving home to go to business on a damp or wet morning is a very elaborate affair. He puts on wash-leather socks over his stockings, and India-rubber shoes above his boots, and wears under his waistcoat a cuirass of hare-skin. Besides these precautions, he winds a thick shawl round his throat, and blocks up his mouth with a large silk handkerchief. Thus accoutred, and furnished besides with a great-coat and umbrella, he braves the dangers of the streets; travelling in severe weather at a gentle trot, the better to preserve the circulation, and bringing his mouth to the surface to take breath, but very seldom, and with the utmost caution. His

The Couple who Coddle themselves

office-door opened, he shoots past his clerk at the same pace, and diving into his own private room, closes the door, examines the window-fastenings, and gradually unrobes himself: hanging his pocket-handkerchief on the fender to air, and determining to write to the newspapers about the fog, which, he says, "has really got to that pitch that it is quite unbearable."

In this last opinion Mrs. Merrywinkle and her respected mother fully concur; for though not present, their thoughts and tongues are occupied with the same subject, which is their constant theme all day. If anybody happens to call, Mrs. Merrywinkle opines that they must assuredly be mad, and her first salutation is, "Why, what in the name of goodness can bring you out in such weather? You know you *must* catch your death." This assurance is corroborated by Mrs. Chopper, who adds, in further confirmation, a dismal legend concerning an individual of her acquaintance who, making a call under precisely parallel circumstances, and being then in the best health and spirits, expired in forty-eight hours afterwards, of a complication of inflammatory disorders. The visitor, rendered not altogether comfortable perhaps by this and other precedents, inquires very affectionately after Mr. Merrywinkle, but by so doing brings about no change of the subject; for Mr. Merrywinkle's name is inseparably connected with his complaints, and his complaints are inseparably connected with Mrs. Merrywinkle's; and when these are done with, Mrs. Chopper, who has been biding her time, cuts in with the chronic disorder—a subject upon which the amiable old lady never leaves off speaking until she is left alone, and very often not then.

But Mr. Merrywinkle comes home to dinner. He is received by Mrs. Merrywinkle and Mrs. Chopper, who, on his remarking that he thinks his feet are damp, turn as pale as ashes and drag him up stairs, imploring him to have them rubbed directly with a dry coarse towel. Rubbed they are, one by Mrs. Merrywinkle and one by Mrs. Chopper, until the friction causes Mr. Merrywinkle to make horrible faces, and look as if he had been smelling very powerful onions; when they desist, and the patient, provided for his better security with thick worsted stockings and list slippers, is borne down stairs to dinner. Now, the dinner is always a good one, the appetites of the diners being delicate, and requiring a little of what Mrs. Merrywinkle calls "tittivation;" the secret of which is understood to lie in good cookery and tasteful spices, and which process is so successfully performed in the present instance, that both Mr. and Mrs. Merrywinkle eat a remarkably good dinner, and even the afflicted Mrs. Chopper wields her knife and fork with much of the spirit and elasticity of youth. But Mr. Merrywinkle, in his desire to gratify his appetite, is not unmindful of his health, for he has a bottle of carbonate of soda with which to qualify his porter, and a little pair of scales in which to weigh it out. Neither in his anxiety to take care of his body is he unmindful of the welfare of his immortal part, as he always prays that for what he is going to receive he may be made truly thankful; and in order that he may be as thankful as possible, eats and drinks to the utmost.

Either from eating and drinking so much, or from being the victim of this constitutional infirmity, among others, Mr. Merrywinkle, after two or three glasses of wine, falls fast asleep; and he has scarcely closed his eyes, when Mrs. Merrywinkle and Mrs. Chopper fall asleep likewise. It is on awakening at tea-time that their most alarming symptoms prevail; for then Mr. Merrywinkle feels as if his temples were tightly bound round with the chain of the street-door, and Mrs. Merrywinkle as if she had made a hearty dinner of half-hundredweights, and Mrs. Chopper as if cold water were running down her back, and oyster-knives with sharp points were plunging of their own accord into her ribs. Symptoms like these are enough to make people peevish, and no wonder that they remain so until supper-time, doing little more than doze and complain, unless Mr. Merrywinkle calls out very loud to a servant "to keep that draught out," or rushes into the passage to flourish his fist in the countenance of the twopenny-postman, for daring to give such a knock as he has just performed, at the door of a private gentleman with nerves.

Supper, coming after dinner, should consist of some gentle provocative; and therefore the tittivating art is again in requisition, and again done honour to by Mr. and Mrs. Merrywinkle, still comforted and abetted by Mrs. Chopper. After supper, it is ten to one but the last-named old lady becomes worse, and is led off to bed with the chronic complaint in full vigour. Mr. and Mrs. Merrywinkle, having administered to her a warm cordial, which is something of the strongest, then repair to their own room, where Mr. Merrywinkle, with his legs and feet in hot water, superintends the mulling of some wine which he is to drink at the very moment he plunges into bed, while Mrs. Merrywinkle, in garments whose nature is unknown to and unimagined by all but married men, takes four small pills with a spasmodic look between each, and finally comes to something hot and fragrant out of another little saucepan, which serves as her composing-draught for the night.

There is another kind of couple who coddle themselves, and who do so at a cheaper rate and on more spare diet, because they are niggardly and parsimonious; for which reason they are kind enough to coddle their visitors too. It is unnecessary to describe them, for our readers may rest assured of the accuracy of these general principles:—that all couples who coddle themselves are selfish and slothful,—that they charge upon every wind that blows, every rain that falls, and every vapour that hangs in the air, the evils which arise from their own imprudence or the gloom which is engendered in their own tempers,—and that all men and women, in couples or otherwise, who fall into exclusive habits of self-indulgence, and forget their natural sympathy and close connexion with everybody and everything in the world around them, not only neglect the first duty of life, but, by a happy retributive justice, deprive themselves of its truest and best enjoyment.

THE OLD COUPLE

THEY are grandfather and grandmother to a dozen grown people and have great-grandchildren besides; their bodies are bent, their hair is grey, their step tottering and infirm. Is this the lightsome pair whose wedding was so merry, and have the young couple indeed grown old so soon?

It seems but yesterday—and yet what a host of cares and griefs are crowded into the intervening time which, reckoned by them, lengthens out into a century! How many new associations have wreathed themselves about their hearts since then! The old time is gone, and a new time has come for others—not for them. They are but the rusting link that feebly joins the two, and is silently loosening its hold and dropping asunder.

It seems but yesterday—and yet three of their children have sunk into the grave, and the tree that shades it has grown quite old. One was an infant—they wept for him; the next a girl, a slight young thing too delicate for earth—her loss was hard indeed to bear. The third, a man. That was the worst of all, but even that grief is softened now.

It seems but yesterday—and yet how the gay and laughing faces of that bright morning have changed and vanished from above ground! Faint likenesses of some remain about them yet, but they are very faint and scarcely to be traced. The rest are only seen in dreams, and even they are unlike what they were, in eyes so old and dim.

One or two dresses from the bridal wardrobe are yet preserved. They are of a quaint and antique fashion, and seldom seen except in pictures. White has turned yellow, and brighter hues have faded. Do you wonder, child? The wrinkled face was once as smooth as yours, the eyes as bright, the shrivelled skin as fair and delicate. It is the work of hands that have been dust these many years.

Where are the fairy lovers of that happy day whose annual return comes upon the old man and his wife, like the echo of some village bell which has long been silent? Let yonder peevish bachelor, racked by rheumatic pains, and quarrelling with the world, let him answer to the question. He recollects something of a favourite playmate; her name was Lucy—so they tell him. He is not sure whether she was married, or went abroad, or died. It is a long while ago, and he don't remember.

Is nothing as it used to be; does no one feel, or think, or act, as in days of yore? Yes. There is an aged woman who once lived servant with the old lady's father, and is sheltered in an alms-house not far off. She is still attached to the family, and loves them all; she nursed the children in her lap, and tended in their sickness those who are no more. Her old mistress has still something of youth in her eyes; the young ladies are like what she was, but not quite so handsome, nor are the gentlemen as stately as Mr. Harvey used to be. She has seen a great deal of trouble; her husband and her son died long ago; but she has got over that, and is happy now—quite happy.

If ever her attachment to her old protectors were disturbed by fresher cares and hopes, it has long since resumed its former current. It has filled the void in the poor creature's heart, and replaced the love of kindred. Death has not left her alone, and this, with a roof above her head, and a warm hearth to sit by, makes her cheerful and contented. Does she remember the marriage of great-grandmamma? Ay, that she does, as well as if it was only yesterday. You wouldn't think it to look at her now, and perhaps she ought not to say so of herself, but she was as smart a young girl then as you'd wish to see. She recollects she took a friend of hers up stairs to see Miss Emma dressed for church; her name was—ah! she forgets the name, but she remembers that she was a very pretty girl, and that she married not long afterwards, and lived—it has quite passed out of her mind where she lived, but she knows she had a bad husband who used her ill, and that she died in Lambeth workhouse. Dear, dear, in Lambeth workhouse!

And the old couple—have they no comfort or enjoyment of existence? See them among their grandchildren and great-grandchildren; how garrulous they are; how they compare one with another, and insist on likenesses which no one else can see; how gently the old lady lectures the girls on

points of breeding and decorum, and points the moral
by anecdotes of herself in her young days—how the old
gentleman chuckles over boyish feats and roguish tricks,
and tells long stores of a "barring-out" achieved at the school
he went to: which was very wrong, he tells the boys, and
never to be imitated of course, but which he cannot help
letting them know was very pleasant too—especially when
he kissed the master's niece. This last, however, is a point on
which the old lady is very tender, for she considers it a
shocking and indelicate thing to talk about, and always says
so whenever it is mentioned, never failing to observe that he
ought to be very penitent for having been so sinful. So the old
gentleman gets no further, and what the schoolmaster's niece
said afterwards (which he is always going to tell) is lost to
posterity.

The old gentleman is eighty years old, to-day—"Eighty
years old, Crofts, and never had a headache," he tells the
barber who shaves him (the barber being a young fellow, and
very subject to that complaint). "That's a great age, Crofts,"
says the old gentleman. "I don't think it's sich a wery great
age, Sir," replies the barber. "Crofts," rejoins the old
gentleman, "you're talking nonsense to me. Eighty not a
great age?" "It's a wery great age, Sir, for a gentleman to be
as healthy and active as you are," returns the barber; "but
my grandfather, Sir, he was ninety-four." "You don't mean
that, Crofts?" says the old gentleman. "I do indeed, Sir,"
retorts the barber, "and as wiggerous as Julius Cæsar, my
grandfather was." The old gentleman muses a little time,
and then says, "What did he die of, Crofts?" "He died
accidentally, Sir," returns the barber; "he didn't mean to do it.
He always would go a running about the streets—walking

never satisfied *his* spirit—and he run against a post and died of a hurt in his chest." The old gentleman says no more until the shaving is concluded, and then he gives Crofts half-a-crown to drink his health. He is a little doubtful of the barber's veracity afterwards, and telling the anecdote to the old lady, affects to make very light of it—though to be sure (he adds) there was old Parr, and in some parts of England, ninety-five or so is a common age— quite a common age.

This morning the old couple are cheerful but serious, recalling old times as well as they can remember them, and dwelling upon many passages in their past lives which the day brings to mind. The old lady reads aloud, in a tremulous voice, out of a great Bible, and the old gentleman with his hand to his ear, listens with profound respect. When the book is closed, they sit silent for a short space, and afterwards resume their conversation, with a reference perhaps to their dead children, as a subject not unsuited to that they have just left. By degrees they are led to consider which of those who survive are the most like those dearly-remembered objects, and so they fall into a less solemn strain, and become cheerful again.

How many people in all, grandchildren, great-grandchildren, and one or two intimate friends of the family, dine together to-day at the eldest son's to congratulate the old couple, and wish them many happy returns, is a calculation beyond our powers; but this we know, that the old couple no sooner present themselves, very sprucely and carefully attired, than there is a violent shouting and rushing forward of the younger branches with all manner of presents, such as pocket-books, pencil-cases, pen-wipers, watch-papers, pin-cushions,

The Old Couple

sleeve-buckles, worked-slippers, watch-guards, and even a nutmeg-grater: the latter article being presented by a very chubby and very little boy, who exhibits it in great triumph as an extraordinary variety. The old couple's emotion at these tokens of remembrance occasions quite a pathetic scene, of which the chief ingredients are a vast quantity of kissing and hugging, and repeated wipings of small eyes and noses with small square pocket-handkerchiefs, which don't come at all easily out of small pockets. Even the peevish bachelor is moved, and he says, as he presents the old gentleman with a queer sort of antique ring from his own finger, that he'll be de'ed if he doesn't think he looks younger than he did ten years ago.

But the great time is after dinner, when the dessert and wine are on the table, which is pushed back to make plenty of room, and they are all gathered in a large circle round the fire, for it is then—the glasses being filled, and everybody ready to drink the toast—that two great-grandchildren rush out at a given signal, and presently return, dragging in old Jane Adams leaning upon her crutched stick, and trembling with age and pleasure. Who so popular as poor old Jane, nurse and story-teller in ordinary to two generations; and who so happy as she, striving to bend her stiff limbs into a curtsey, while tears of pleasure steal down her withered cheeks!

The old couple sit side by side, and the old time seems like yesterday indeed. Looking back upon the path they have travelled, its dust and ashes disappear; the flowers that withered long ago, show brightly again upon its borders, and they grow young once more in the youth of those about them.

CONCLUSION

———◆———

WE have taken for the subjects of the foregoing moral essays, twelve samples of married couples, carefully selected from a large stock on hand, open to the inspection of all comers. These samples are intended for the benefit of the rising generation of both sexes, and, for their more easy and pleasant information, have been separately ticketed and labelled in the manner they have seen.

We have purposely excluded from consideration the couple in which the lady reigns paramount and supreme, holding such cases to be of a very unnatural kind, and like hideous births and other monstrous deformities, only to be discreetly and sparingly exhibited.

And here our self-imposed task would have ended, but that to those young ladies and gentlemen who are yet revolving singly round the church, awaiting the advent of that time when the mysterious laws of attraction shall draw them towards it in couples, we are desirous of addressing a few last words.

Before marriage and afterwards, let them learn to centre all their hopes of real and lasting happiness in their own fireside; let them cherish the faith that in home, and all the English virtues which the love of home engenders, lies the only true source of domestic felicity; let them believe that round the household gods, contentment and tranquillity cluster in their gentlest and most graceful forms; and that many weary hunters of happiness through the noisy world, have learnt this truth too late, and found a cheerful spirit and a quiet mind only at home at last.

How much may depend on the education of daughters and the conduct of mothers; how much of the brightest part of our old national character may be perpetuated by their wisdom or frittered away by their folly—how much of it may have been lost already, and how much more in danger of vanishing every day—are questions too weighty for discussion here, but well deserving a little serious consideration from all young couples nevertheless.

To that one young couple on whose bright destiny the thoughts of nations are fixed, may the youth of England look, and not in vain, for an example. From that one young couple, blessed and favoured as they are, may they learn that even the glare and glitter of a court, the splendour of a palace, and the pomp and glory of a throne, yield in their power of conferring happiness to domestic worth and virtue. From that one young couple may they learn that the crown of a great empire, costly and jewelled though it be, gives place in the estimation of a Queen to the plain gold ring that links her woman's nature to that of tens of thousands of her humble subjects, and guards in her woman's heart one secret store of tenderness, whose proudest boast shall be that it knows no Royalty save Nature's own, and no pride of birth but being the child of heaven!

So shall the highest young couple in the land for once hear the truth, when men throw up their caps, and cry with loving shouts—

GOD BLESS THEM.